Gossip

Gossip
The Evil Stepmother's Tale

Cay Templeton
Edited By: Allegra Wilson

AuthorHouse™
1663 Liberty Drive
Bloomington, IN 47403
www.authorhouse.com
Phone: 1-800-839-8640

© 2012 by Cay Templeton. All rights reserved.

No part of this book may be reproduced, stored in a retrieval system, or transmitted by any means without the written permission of the author.

Published by AuthorHouse   03/06/2012

ISBN: 978-1-4685-5437-3 (sc)
ISBN: 978-1-4685-5436-6 (e)

Library of Congress Control Number: 2012903156

Any people depicted in stock imagery provided by Thinkstock are models, and such images are being used for illustrative purposes only. Certain stock imagery © Thinkstock.

This book is printed on acid-free paper.

Because of the dynamic nature of the Internet, any web addresses or links contained in this book may have changed since publication and may no longer be valid. The views expressed in this work are solely those of the author and do not necessarily reflect the views of the publisher, and the publisher hereby disclaims any responsibility for them.

For Mom and DJ
&
All Stepmothers who have been misunderstood.

Special Thanks

God
Family & Friends
Allegra Wilson
Krista Leitzke
Christina Cordle
Dawn Anderson
Ken Vose
Jacob Appleberg
Robert Christie
Sophie Marie
And of course . . . Humbug

Contents

Chapter 1	"Gossip"	1
Chapter 2	"Count Daughtry"	8
Chapter 3	"Midnight Visitor"	19
Chapter 4	"Dragons, Ales, Fairies, & Tales"	26
Chapter 5	"Whirlwind Adventures"	34
Chapter 6	"Locked Doors"	42
Chapter 7	"The Little Cinder Girl"	48
Chapter 8	"Squeaky Clean"	57
Chapter 9	"Integral Part"	65
Chapter 10	"Victor Krouse"	72
Chapter 11	"The Evil Fairy Godmother"	79
Chapter 12	"Best Of Friends"	88
Chapter 13	"Late Night Stroll"	96

Chapter 14	"Clean Hands"	105
Chapter 15	"The King's Mistress"	112
Chapter 16	"The Queen's Tale"	120
Chapter 17	"The Masked Ball"	130
Chapter 18	"The Secret Artist"	140
Chapter 19	"Puzzle Pieces"	146
Chapter 20	"The Cane"	154
Chapter 21	"Happy Endings"	166

Chapter 1
"Gossip"

Gossip, by definition, is to talk idly about others' affairs, and it tends, at times, to be quite cruel. It would seem to be the case in this particular town, at this particular time that the harshest gossip revolved around the Queen's evil stepmother, the Countess De Leon. She has always been described as a hard-nosed woman whose sole aspiration in life was for her eldest daughter to marry the prince.

Seldom did anyone ever see the Countess in court or even in town for that matter. But on the rare visits she did make, most noted that she always carried a walking stick. It was the 'staff of terror,' as the town's children called it. Many say that, outside of walking, its main purpose was to beat her stepdaughter anytime she failed to complete her chores on time. As the gossip goes, Isabella, also known in this tale as Cinderella, was forced to wash all the clothes, scrub every floor, dust the tapestries and tend to all yard work. At the day's end, the young girl was locked up in the tower to be kept out of sight and out of thought.

Of course, no one ever witnessed the Countess' alleged cruelty. The only evidence that remained was the scars on the Queen's body and the speculative gossip that would taunt the Countess for years. Once Isabella was married to Prince Fabian, the Countess De Leon went into hiding on her estate, where she has remained ever since.

That is, until a most peculiar invitation was delivered into the hands of Mademoiselle Claire Du Bois to come visit her...

* * *

"Whoa," escaped Claire's lips as she looked out the carriage window. Even with the long shadows of dusk, the magnificence of the Countess De Leon's lavish home was unmistakable. The large, two-story home rested a little way off the main country road. Acres upon acres of not just open land, but also forest went in every direction.

Without warning, the coach door flew open, and the cool evening breeze swept through the compartment. Just outside the door, an older man cordially bowed to Claire.

"Welcome, Mademoiselle Du Bois. I am Botley, the head butler here at the Countess De Leon's home."

He extended his hand to her, coaxing her out of the carriage. Once on solid ground, Claire couldn't help but notice the stone wall as it stood menacingly, encompassing the Countess' estate.

"We are quite pleased to see that you have made it safely," he said as Claire's eyes landed on the rotund figure before her.

"It is a true honor to be invited," said Claire, bowing her head with thanks.

"If I might ask, my lady, where is your escort? Surely you did not travel all the way from Stuttgart alone," Botley inquired with mild concern.

"Most of my travel I was escorted by my dear friend, Victor Krouse. He took leave to visit a sick aunt in Chartres but he will be joining me in town tomorrow."

"I see," Botley murmured. "Well, while you are here with us, I hope you will find your accommodations to be comfortable and to your liking."

Judging by his pleasant smile, he seemed to be filled with some inexplicable delight at her being there. She didn't let that distract her.

"My stay here?" Claire repeated. "I thought I might stay in town. After all, I do not get the chance to travel much outside of Germany."

Botley's happiness dwindled as if he knew something she did not. But before Claire had a chance to say another word on the matter, he gestured to the grand staircase before them. "After you, Mademoiselle."

"What is this all about, Botley?" Claire asked. "I received the most curious invitation from the Countess De Leon."

"I could not say, Mademoiselle."

The old butler continued holding his gesture to the stairs, unrelenting in letting Claire go anywhere but forward.

"Botley!" came a stark voice. "Mother is waiting."

Botley didn't bother to look, but Claire turned to see the young woman whose thin frame was silhouetted in the front door.

"*Oui*, Lady Genevieve," Botley replied.

Without another word, Genevieve disappeared back into the house.

"I do apologize, the Countess wishes to see you at once. This way, please."

Botley turned and hurried up through the front door.

"Botley wait, who was that?" she shouted, quickly following him. "Botley?"

Crossing over the threshold, Claire lost her thought completely. The entrance hall was even more glorious than the front of the home. To either side was a staircase that led up to the upstairs halls with intricately carved railings that were encased in gold. Overhead was a domed ceiling that displayed gods riding chariots across a cloudy sky.

Botley didn't hesitate before scuttling up the right staircase. Claire became breathless by the old butler's quick pace.

Stepping into the upstairs hallway, Claire instantly noticed the large bay windows facing away from the front of the house. Much to her dismay, when she looked out, nothing could be seen through the darkness.

"That is the Countess' private garden, Mademoiselle," Botley mentioned. "All four walls of the house surround it so that she might enjoy the outdoors undisturbed."

"The house is built around it?" she asked, trying to understand the unique architecture of this strange yet fascinating home.

"Yes."

Botley moved next to Claire and mimicked her gaze out the window. "She so loves her flowers. They come from all over the world, you know?"

"She must have quite a fortune to be able to afford such a Utopia," Claire stated, keeping her focus forward.

"She does," agreed the old butler. "But in all fairness, the Countess brought most of her plants back with her when she returned from her holidays with the Count."

At this, Claire broke and looked at Botley. "The Count. Seldom does anyone ever mention him. Was he a good sort of man?"

"The best," Botley said as his face softened into a pleasant smile again. "If you wish, I would be happy to show you the garden tomorrow once the sun has come up."

"I would very much enjoy that," Claire said, contentedly.

Botley nodded his head to finalize the agreement, then spun on his heel and continued down the hall.

Entering the last hall, they drew close to the Countess' study when Claire stopped dead in her tracks. Hanging on the wall was a huge portrait of a young woman who sat gracefully in her chair with a humorous smile. Her very graceful stature demanded the attention of every passerby.

"Is this-" Claire stopped.

"Isabella's mother, Mademoiselle."

"The Queen's mother?" Claire repeated, a little confused.

"Yes. She passed away while giving birth to her."

Claire began to gnaw on her lower lip while she studied the entirety of the young woman's face.

"How old was the Queen when the Count remarried?" Claire inquired.

"Five years after her mother died, I think," Botley said, taking a closer look at the painting himself.

"Why would the Countess keep this up in the hall; next to her study, no less? It does not seem right."

Botley seemed to choose his words carefully before he said, "In the many years that I have served the Countess, I have learned two things. One, the Countess always has a reason for everything she does, and two, I do not always know what it is."

Frustration and confusion whirled around Claire the more she studied the pale pinks and beige colors that were used in composing the woman's face. Her eyes flickered between the portrait and its closeness to the Countess' study door. At last, her eyebrows lifted and her face relaxed.

"I see," she said knowingly.

A light-hearted chuckle came from behind her.

"You were perfectly chosen for this, Mademoiselle Du Bois," boasted Botley.

"This?" said Claire, trying to get any hint of what he was referring to.

"You just figured out why the Countess put this painting right outside her door. Did you not?"

Claire bit her lower lip while her face contorted at the question. "I believe I know why, but it is all speculation."

Botley nodded his head approvingly. "I hear you are quite the sleuth."

"You could say it is a hobby of mine."

Botley walked over to the Countess' study door and opened it. "Let us see where this hobby leads you while you are here."

Claire looked into a dark room that lay just beyond the doorway, questioning if anyone was even in there. Her expression soured the more she allowed her mind to run wild with why the Countess invited her there.

"You did not come all this way to stop now, did you? The Countess De Leon has not spoken to anyone since Isabella was made Queen. You should take it as an honor that she asked you into her home."

Claire's shoulders dropped, acknowledging he was in fact correct on all accounts. Going through that door was the only way she would get answers to the mounting questions that continued to fill her mind.

"Will you be here when I am finished?"

"Of course, my lady."

Drawing closer to the door, Claire could feel the thumping in her chest growing stronger.

"She has been waiting a long time to see you," Botley said as he nodded his head for her to go in.

Claire was perplexed by the remark but didn't let it stop her from plunging head long into the darkness.

Chapter 2

"Count Daughtry"

Once the study door was closed behind her, Claire had to feel around to make her way through the room. Her eyes strained to compose the outline of each object she passed. An odd odor permeated the air and grew stronger with every step she took. All of a sudden, her knee slammed into a small table and she heard glass smashing on the floor.

"Oh, blast it all," she grumbled, and then leaned over to feel around for the broken pieces.

"Leave it," said a husky voice.

The hair on the back of Claire's neck stood on end. A glowing red ember danced through the air a few feet in front of her.

"Countess De Leon?"

In only a moment's time a spark flew and a flame was flickering at the tip of a wick. The Countess De Leon lit several candles while she stood prominently behind her overly large desk. Even with the little light that was produced, Claire could still make out the hard, yet refined, face of the older woman smoking a hand-carved pipe.

Gossip

Her clothes were of fine fabrics and her salt and peppered color hair was tightly wrapped into a spinster's bun. The only thing that jumped out immediately was the dark crevices that were embedded underneath her eyes.

"You really needn't bother with that," said the Countess.

Transfixed by the woman, Claire left the shattered figurine on the floor and moved to the armchair in front of the desk. Both the Countess and she sat simultaneously down in their chairs.

Breaking free from the intense stare, Claire allowed her eyes to survey the room, taking note of every detail. The floor-to-ceiling bookshelves that covered three out of four walls of the study were the first thing that captured her attention. Not even if she read for five years straight did she think she could get through all these classics that hailed from every corner of the world.

"I have no doubts that you are wondering why I have brought you here, Mademoiselle Du Bois."

"I am curious," agreed Claire, her eyes landing on the portrait of the Count and the Countess with three little girls sitting at their feet. Two of the girls sat closer to the front of the picture while the third girl hid behind her father's breeches.

"Well, I have no need to beat around the bush about this," said the Countess sternly, demanding Claire's attention.

"It seems to me that I have been very . . ." The Countess' lips pursed, quenching her pipe between them. ". . . misunderstood by everyone."

"Honestly, Countess De Leon, I do not see how I can help you with the matter."

"Oh, come, come now. Surely, you of all people know how you can help me."

The Countess' eyes narrowed in delight. The weighted meaning behind her words hit Claire hard.

"Me?" Claire stammered.

"You are not just clever when it comes to solving mysteries, but you are also capable of writing it all down," said the Countess decisively. "I want the people out there to know my side of the Queen's very twisted story."

"Is that why you brought me here? You want to tell me your story?" Claire retorted through her fingers that were sprawled across her lips, still taking in the situation unfolding before her.

"I need someone who will not be swayed by politics or bullying from the Queen. Someone who can understand what it is like to be an outcast. For that is what I have become ever since . . ."

The Countess trailed off. Claire noticed the Countess' face drain of color before she looked away. An awkward moment of silence fell between the two women.

"Is the Baron Dupree still in hiding?" The Countess asked.

Before she digested what the Countess had asked, Claire could feel the heat rising in her cheeks. Instead of backing down from the question, she locked eyes with the stern woman sitting across from her. "Clearly not."

The Countess smiled, pleased with herself. "I was hoping that he and his . . . 'protégé' would hear me," she said, gesturing to Claire.

"Under one condition."

"You want to know how I found out that he was your nom de plume," the Countess blurted out.

Claire cocked her head to one side, acknowledging the Countess' question.

"If you stay until the end, I promise you will learn how I found out you were writing under that name."

Another awkward moment of silence passed between them while the two women measured each other's intentions. The tension was thick but not as strong as the curiosity swarming around the Countess' words. Clearly, this woman was not someone to be trifled with. And as much as Claire was astute to details that led her to solving problems, in her current predicament she was at a loss.

Reaching down into her satchel, Claire grabbed some parchment, a quill, and a little bottle of ink.

"Where would you like to begin?"

"At the beginning, of course," the Countess said in short.

"The beginning," Claire repeated, scribbling the words down.

The Countess' eyes drifted down to a small picture frame that sat on her desk. All Claire could see was the back of the canvas stretched cleanly over the wooden frame. Though she wondered what had captured the Countess' undivided attention, she dared not ask.

"The fireworks were grand that year. Festivities were in full swing on the eve of Prince Fabian's seventh birthday. Of course, as you know, he is now the King."

Claire dropped her head in acknowledgement and waited for the Countess to continue.

"People showed up in masses at the castle to drink and have a merry time. I, on the other hand, had no desire to be there at all. It is a wonder that I ever went."

"Why?" Claire blurted out.

The Countess paused for a moment. Her ice blue eyes shot up. "If you will allow me to finish."

Claire nodded, a little embarrassed. "Of course. Please, go on."

"My husband passed away and it had been hard times for my two daughters and myself. Genevieve was especially close to her father and I would almost venture to say that she took his death the hardest. I would have much preferred to stay home and ease her to sleep than go to some ridiculous ball.

"When it came to festivities, I wanted nothing to do with them. However, my dear friend, Lady Devereaux, thought it might be good for me to get out into society again. She was not a woman to take "no" for an answer.

"I had not put much effort into my attire that night, for whom was I trying to impress? But when I climbed out of the carriage, I saw a man who instantly made me regret my decision.

"Count Daughtry was a handsome man to be sure and the talk of all of France. Actually, you could say he was the talk of Europe seeing that he was a charming businessman who traveled to all over the world for his work. I personally had never met him but could tell by the flock of young lady admirers standing around him that he was considered the most eligible bachelor in all of France."

Claire found her whole body had slid to the edge of the chair as she had become more entranced by the Countess' story. Biting her lower lip, she asked, "Did you join his circle?"

"Certainly not," snapped the Countess. "He could have had any young lady he wanted with his vast estates.

I found it difficult to believe he would even glance in my direction."

"But he did."

Just for a moment, Claire could see a little smile crack at the corner of Countess De Leon's lips. No matter how slight or fleeting the moment was, Claire could tell the Countess had truly enjoyed being with the Count.

"I was standing in a secluded corner for a long time and simply wanted to go home. Then a carnation appeared over my shoulder. I was not sure what was going on at first, but when I turned, there stood Count Daughtry with his charming smile.

"'Loveliness of this kind should not be hidden in dark corners,' he said to me and then kissed my hand. Even now, I can remember my face flushing red. I turned away so he would not see how embarrassed I was.

"I used smelling the flower as a diversion so I could compose myself. I turned back to him and said, 'Thank you for the flower,' but he had gone."

"Where?" asked Claire.

"Back to the group of fawning admirers, no doubt. I spent the rest of that evening alone, watching people enjoy themselves in a way that I could not.

"By the time my carriage pulled up, I was thankful to be going home. Much to my surprise, when the door swung open, there was someone else in *my* carriage."

"'Get out of my carriage at once,' I demanded. But the figure did not move. 'Who do you think you are? Get out of my carriage.'

"Lord Devereaux came up behind me and asked, 'Is everything alright here?'

"'Certainly not!' I replied. 'This man will not remove himself from my carriage.'

"Lord Devereaux stepped closer. 'You there, get out of the Countess' carriage. Why are you trying to stir up trouble here?'

"'My humblest apologies,' came a deep voice that demanded attention at the very sound of it.

"'Count Daughtry. I am sorry, sir. You seemed to have startled Countess De Leon,' said Lord Devereaux. I was speechless. How could Lord Devereaux be apologizing to the riff raff who was in *my* carriage? At that point I was furious. I shoved Lord Devereaux out of the way and looked in and yelled, 'You need to come out of there at once!'

"I thought a great many things were going to happen but nothing could have prepared me for this."

Claire's hand had stopped writing and her eyes were fixed on the Countess as she spoke.

"He reached out his gloved hand and offered me a ride."

"How romantic," Claire breathed.

"Romantic? I was not romanced. I was irate, insulted, and what made it worse was the charming smile that accompanied his foolishness. 'This sort of thing may work with all those girls who follow you around but it certainly will not work with me,' I screamed at him.

"'My lady, I simply wish you to take a ride with me. Is there any harm in that?'

"Before I had time to reject his offer, Lord Devereaux came up behind me and said, 'Desiree, this will do you some good.' And he shoved me into the back seat and slammed the door behind me."

"The whole evening sounds fascinating," Claire blurted out.

"I am sure many young ladies found his games humorous," Countess De Leon replied. "I personally thought him a rogue. Fooling me at the ball into believing that he was a charming man, and there he was, kidnapping me with my own carriage."

"Maybe he thought you would be more comfortable?"

"I am sure he had his reasons, however sordid they were."

The Countess redirected her eyes from the picture on her desk up to Claire. It seemed pretty apparent that something of great importance was occupying her mind. Her lower lips began to quiver.

"Are you all right, Countess?" Claire asked softly. "Countess?"

"I did not know what to make of him at first. He was the most unpredictable man." She reached out and picked up the picture, no longer resisting the temptation to touch it.

"The reason I brought you here, Mademoiselle Du Bois, is to tell you of my time with Isabella. If nothing else happens during our time together, it is imperative that you understand what *I* went through . . . what *I* was faced with when I raised her."

Claire left the paper on the desk and leaned back in her chair. Studying the Countess' face, she could see the years of strain and torment etched in her eyes.

"What is it you wish to tell me, Countess De Leon?"

"Despite what lies my stepdaughter has spread about me, I cared very much for her father. As I did for her."

"She tells tales of you whipping her."

"I know."

"Tales of you making her clean all the house by herself and living up in the tower."

"I know."

"She had to go to town almost every day to get the food and run the errands while you relaxed at your lavish home."

The Countess slammed her hand down on the desk. "Mademoiselle Du Bois, you are here to correct those lies!"

"There are even rumors that you constantly mocked her cinder-covered clothes by calling her Cinderella."

The Countess' head retracted, and her jaw line became distinguished as she clenched her teeth. Claire knew that she had not said anything false.

"It happened once. But in a world such as this, that is all it takes." The Countess rose from her chair and turned to the window behind her desk. Looking out at the star-covered sky, she sighed.

Claire noticed that there was an object . . . a painting leaning against the wall by the Countess, but when the Countess realized Claire was looking at it she immediately turned it around.

"Do you want to know what I think of my stepdaughter?"

Trying to decipher the Countess' odd behavior, Claire remained silently waiting for the answer.

"She is a confused girl who wants nothing more than her mother and her father to be alive again. Because I could not give that to her, she hates me."

"It is not easy being a stepmother, is it?" asked Claire, caringly.

The Countess De Leon dropped her head and struggled to speak. "No," she whispered. "No, it is not."

"Do you wish to continue?'

The Countess turned to Claire with a half smile. "I do, but not tonight. I am tired."

She grabbed a little golden bell sitting on the corner of her desk and rang it. Not a second had passed before Botley came in. The old butler bowed and gestured with his hands for Claire to follow him out.

"What about your story?'

"Tomorrow."

"All right," Claire said, disappointed in having to stop so abruptly. "I will be back here first thing in the morning so that we can get an early start."

"You will not be coming back."

"I beg your pardon?"

"You will not need to come back because you will be staying here."

"I have already made arrangements to stay in town. I have some business there, you see."

"Maybe you have not started to comprehend the severity of your decision to visit me, Mademoiselle Du Bois, but you will now be considered a conspirator against the Queen of France."

"That is ridiculous!"

"Is it? Everyone in town knows that you are here. After all, how many carriages do you think I receive? You will be placed in prison and probably not heard from again."

"That seems rather harsh, do you not think?"

"I will be the first to attest that all it takes is one false accusation, and you will disappear like that." The Countess snapped her fingers with the close of her remark. Claire's eyes refocused on them. Her heart started to race and she could feel her stomach drop.

"I think it safest for you to remain within these walls," the Countess concluded.

"Who is to say no one will come on your land to get me, or *you*?"

"This land has a lot of significance to the Queen. She was raised here and all her memories of her father are here. She knows that all it would take is one little match and everything would be destroyed like that."

"You would do that?"

"I will do whatever it takes to survive. She has pushed me that far."

"I have underestimated you, Countess De Leon, and the situation you find yourself in."

The Countess' eyes narrowed and a slight sneer creased her lips.

"This little misfortune you now find yourself in, Mademoiselle Du Bois, is only the beginning of the hell I have been subjected to for the past several years."

Chapter 3
"Midnight Visitor"

Claire moved at a slow pace as she passed through the halls toward her unwanted bedchamber. Thoughts of being hauled off to prison to never be heard from again weighed heavily on her mind.

"She is a good woman, the Countess De Leon," Botley said softly. "I know you might feel like she misguided you."

"She trapped me," Claire corrected him.

"She knows what she is doing," Botley finished, keeping the same slow pace along side her. "When the time comes for you to return to Germany, she will make sure you get there safely."

Claire looked over skeptically at the old butler. He didn't return the look but instead kept his focus forward at the hall in front of him.

"I am glad you are confident," Claire finally said.

"I have known the Countess for many years now. She does not do anything without thinking it through first, and if she has had anything in the last several years, it is time to think."

Claire's head dropped, "I wish that could console me."

Botley stopped abruptly, while Claire took a few more steps past him. She thought that the wise old butler was about to give her a comforting speech about having faith that everything would work out in the end. Much to her surprise, when she turned back to him, he was creeping suspiciously to a closed door off to the side of the hall.

"What on Earth?" Claire uttered.

Botley pressed his finger to his lips to silence her, and then put his ear to the door, listening. Claire moved next to him and leaned forward to listen too. But before her ear could connect with the wood, Botley threw the door open and leapt into the room, screaming, "Ah, ha!"

Claire stepped backward, startled by his odd behavior. A brief moment passed when she thought Botley had lost his mind, which would seem fitting considering that this whole family had been exiled to this house for quite some time. But the old butler was not crazy. Less than a second later she heard a heap of giggles, easing her concern.

Claire straightened up and wiped her dress methodically, trying to regain her composure, when Botley came back out into the hall.

"Is everything all right?" she asked, more composed.

"Of course," he said with a smirk, continuing down the hall as if nothing peculiar just happened.

"Wait a moment," Claire said, chasing him down. "What happened just now?"

"Oh, that? That was only Josephine. She likes to play hide and seek a lot."

"And you found her?"

"I did. She has been hiding for the better part of the day, but I heard a floorboard creak. Deductive reasoning says it was not Lady Genevieve. So, I figured I had found Josephine's hiding spot."

"Very clever. Just one question: how did you reach the conclusion that it was not Lady Genevieve?"

"Because, that room is Count Daughtry's painting room, and Isabella spent a great deal of time in there when she was a child. Not wanting to recount old memories, Lady Genevieve stays away from there."

With a complex look firmly planted on her face, Claire nodded her head, trying to follow the old butler's logic.

"I see. Maybe you took up the wrong profession, Herr Botley. You might have made a right fine detective."

Botley shook his head. "I do not know about that. I still have one or two unfinished mysteries of my own that demand my attention right now."

"I have no doubt that you will figure it all out."

"I do hope so. The key to being a great inquisitor is to pay attention to details. For instance, how is it that you come from Germany but you bear a French name? It is very intriguing to me."

She felt her lower lip curl under her teeth while a small sigh escaped.

"It is not an interesting story, to be honest. My mother left France just before I was born. Mother said that my father was lost on the high seas and staying in our home in France was far too painful for her to bear."

"I see," said Botley, his voice much softer than before.

Claire stopped and looked into his pale eyes.

"Are you all right?"

"Yes, of course," he said, clearing his throat. "Now, here is your room," he said and gestured to the door off to the left of the hall. "Your lady's maids will be in there to help ready you for bed."

"Thank you," Claire said and pushed her way into the bedroom. "I wish you a goodnight."

"Goodnight, my dear," Botley said with a courteous bow.

* * *

For the time that Claire fretted her unwanted stay at the Countess' home, she didn't seem to mind the large bed that could easily have fit a small family in it. She let her head fall unhindered onto one of the four feather pillows. Stretching her legs to their fullest extent, she was pleased that they didn't even cover half the length of the bed.

With one strong puff, she blew out the single candle lit on her elegant nightstand, and then buried her face deep into the comfort of her fluffy pillows.

The stillness of night settled in. Claire had to admit that these accommodations were far superior to the small inn in town.

Just when her eyes grew heavy and dreams were only seconds away; she heard something creak open that caused her to reawaken in alarm. She remained motionless except for her hand that she lifted to her lips to stifle her heavy breathing. The intruder could be heard, step by step, moving toward the bed.

All of a sudden the person was upon her. She attempted to scream but a soft, petite hand quickly covered her mouth.

"Shh."

The candle next to the bed lit again.

"Fräulein Genevieve?" Claire forced out of her quivering lips. "You gave me a fright."

The hooded figure sat with great propriety next to her on the bed. A single golden lock that rested on the jade-colored cloak was the only hint as to who the intruder was. Genevieve looked up, allowing the candlelight to catch her face properly.

Claire sat up, resting her back against the headboard and taking a deep breath to calm her nerves.

"Fräulein, it is a pleasure to finally meet you. I do apologize that I am not more suitably dressed for such an occasion."

A contented smile crossed Genevieve's pouty lips. "I am sorry to be calling on you like this," she finally said. "I know it is not customary to talk at such a late hour and Mother would be furious if she knew that I was bothering her guest after you traveled such a long way."

Claire looked past Genevieve to the painting that was turned inward into the wall and the secret passage that lay just beyond it.

"It is no trouble. I was hoping that I would get to speak with you at some point during my unexpected stay here."

Genevieve pulled the hood away from her head allowing all her hair to fall freely down her back and around her face. She looked even more picturesque now that Claire was able to see her more closely. Her little button nose led up to her thin brow, and her forest-green eyes shone brightly against her fair skin.

"I am quite aware that my mother brought you here to talk about her time with Isabella."

"Tricked was more like what she did," Claire pointed out.

"Please understand, she had no other choice."

"That seems to be everyone else's opinion as well. So, let me ask you a pressing question. What is it you need that could not wait until morning?"

Genevieve's head cocked to one side as she studied Claire closely. The weighty stare allowed Claire to see the similarities between the Countess and her daughter. The same determined chin and exhaustion was present in the crevices under her eyes.

"What I need to ask has nothing to do with Isabella, but another matter entirely.

"All right. I am listening."

Genevieve's eyes softened and she took Claire's hand. "This tale is far too lengthy to tell you now, but I wanted to see if I could steal you away for a short time in the morning. We can meet in the garden."

"I do very much wish to see the garden," Claire said enthusiastically. Then her eyes shot back up to Genevieve. "I cannot, I am to meet with your mother in the morning."

"She can wait."

"But-"

"She has waited this long, what is a little longer?" said Genevieve rising from the bed and placing the cloak back over her head. "Please say you will come."

"I will try."

"Thank you," she whispered, sounding relieved and almost giddy.

Before Claire knew it, Genevieve disappeared back through the secret entranceway and restored the painting to its rightful place on the wall.

Claire lay for a moment longer looking up at the canopy of her bed. "So, I have a Countess who wants to falsify the Queen's story, an old butler who plays hide and seek in the most unusual ways, a young woman who wants to steal more of my time, and I might end up in prison and disappear forever," she said, just before blowing out the candle once more. "What have I gotten myself into here?"

Chapter 4
"Dragons, Ales, Fairies, & Tales"

The early morning light came flooding through the bedchamber window and rested perfectly on Claire's face, waking her. At first, she had forgotten where she was, but then the unforgettable trapped feeling rushed over her.

She tried to close her eyes again, but the heat from the sun's rays beckoned her to remain awake.

"Ugh," she growled.

When her eyes fluttered open, she noticed something on the canopy that she hadn't the night before: a picture. A classic picture of a knight riding up to a castle to rescue his fair maiden in the tower was sewn intricately into the fabric. Being that it was the same color tone as the rest of the canopy, it was understandable how she could have easily missed it the night before.

Her eyes scoured over the picture with such fine precision that allowed her mind to churn. Then finally, her eyes fixated on the tower.

"Of course."

Gossip

* * *

The coolness of the floor helped push Claire's eager feet forward as she glided from hallway to endless hallway unaware of how to get where she was going. Not even the curiosity of the secret garden outside the sun-filled windows slowed her down.

She hastened her step until her body froze in front of a worn wooden door. When she went for the handle, it took her full weight to heave the door open. The cool air funneled down the spiral stone staircase, giving her a slight chill.

"This is it," she whispered under her breath.

Claire took her first step up the tower stairs, when she heard a throat clearing.

"My goodness, Herr Botley. You scared me," she said, with her hand on her chest, startled.

Botley stood with his hands neatly tucked behind his back and one of his eyebrows raised inquisitively.

"I would ask, Mademoiselle Du Bois, what it is you are doing, but I already know the answer. So, instead I will ask why you feel a need to go through Her Majesty's possessions?"

"Please understand, Herr Botley, the Countess is about to tell me years of her life with the Queen. If I cannot see with my own eyes where the Queen grew up, I will not know if the Countess is fabricating the truth or if her story is indeed honest."

"Ever the detective."

"I knew you would understand," Claire said, taking another step up.

"Perhaps I could show you another place where the Queen spent far more of her time than the tower."

Claire instantly noticed Botley's softhearted smile that accompanied his remark.

"What kind of a place?"

"A dark, dank one. Full of all kinds of surprises," he said in a mysterious voice.

"Intriguing, but is it enough?" Claire stepped up the staircase and out of sight.

"I can show you something that not even the Countess knows about."

In an instant, Claire reappeared in front of the old butler.

"All right, you have my attention."

Botley simply turned on his heel and began walking down the hallway away from her. Claire didn't even stop to think before running after him.

"Herr Botley, where are we going? Herr Botley?"

His only response to her was a quickened pace before turning down another hall. The two made their way down a narrow stone stair that led into a dark room. A dense smoke smell slightly outweighed the musty dank one.

"Where are we?"

A match struck and a fire roared in the fireplace.

"This cannot be . . ." Her hand covered her mouth in awe.

Botley started feeling against the stone hearth. Claire squinted her eyes, struggling to see what he was doing.

"Ah." Botley sputtered.

He pulled a medium-sized stone out of the wall. Behind it rested an old book, which looked to be in good condition. Botley slid the stone back into place and sat down at the child-sized wooden table in the middle of the room. Claire joined him.

"Seldom do we know why things happen the way they do."

Claire looked anxiously at Botley, not knowing what he meant.

"The Countess De Leon cannot fathom how a dirty little child could grow up to be Queen. Just like the Queen could not figure out why her father died while she was so young, leaving her here alone."

Claire rested back in the tiny wooden chair, listening to Botley's every word.

"This is the last book the Queen was given by her father before he died. We read it together for a short time, and then she began to read it on her own. She was a very gifted child despite her oddities. I am hoping, by giving you this, that it will help you understand a little more about who she really was."

Botley placed the pocket-sized book on the table and slowly slid it across to Claire. She gently placed her hands down on the hard cover. Sliding her thumb through the cinders, the title became visible. The gold lettering embossed on the front read: "Dragons, Ales, Fairies, and Tales."

Opening the book up, the pages at the beginning were in pristine condition. The paper was still bright white and not a single wrinkle or smudge affected the lettering. But as Claire thumbed through to the middle, the pages became worn so thin that it was hard to make out the pictures and some of the corners were torn.

Backtracking through the chapter, it was made evident that the section that was so thoroughly read was the Fairy stories.

"I would suggest you read this chapter first before bringing it up to the Countess. This book is, how should

I say, a sensitive subject for her. She believes that it was destroyed when the Queen left."

"Why would she think that?"

"Because she asked me to do it and I am usually an obedient servant."

Claire looked back down to the book in her hands. "So why did you not?"

"I cared about Isabella's wellbeing long before the Countess ever came to live with us. Her happiness was important to me. So, I hid the book in our secret hiding place where no one could find it except for her and myself."

For a moment Claire could swear that Botley's eyes were becoming teary but he stood up too quickly for her to be sure.

"I will give you a little time before I take you to the Countess' study."

Claire nodded, dismissing Botley, and then turned her attention back to the book in front of her. In big golden letters across the page, the title read, "The Fairy Queen." Sliding her finger over the picture, many of them looked familiar. A little girl was sleeping upon a pile of hay in the corner of a barn. An evil witch was forcing the little girl to clean the house and cook the food. If she did not do her tasks accordingly, she would be whipped with a cane.

Page after page, the story read so familiarly. The witch once was so angry at the girl that she took a bolt of lightning from the sky and struck down the girl's father as punishment. After so much torment, the girl prayed for some relief from her horrible situation. One night, the Fairy Queen came to her while she was sleeping. She gave the girl a small purse of money and changed the girl's whole appearance. The new appearance allowed the young girl to sneak out right under the evil witch's nose. When the witch found out that she had been outsmarted by this little girl, she became so enraged that she exploded into a bunch of little pieces. The little girl eventually married the prince and they lived happily ever after.

Claire closed the book after finishing the tale. "I see," she said to herself.

"What we can see with great clarity is that what must be shall be," sang an unexpected voice behind her.

Startled, Claire spun in her chair to see a slender figure lingering in the doorway. Unlike Genevieve, however, Josephine's frame lacked the discipline to stand up straight and her head was dropped.

"Are you Fräulein Josephine?"

"Never can I say what has gone astray."

The shadows made it almost impossible to see the odd girl with any clarity. It wasn't until she moved into the firelight that Claire caught a glimpse of the aimlessness in Josephine's eyes through the long stringy hair that rested over her face.

"Fräulein Josephine?"

The girl did not stop at the table but instead danced past it. Walking to the fireplace, she stared at the hearth with great interest.

"How could you know when things cannot grow? They will die just as fast as a sigh."

Her fingers explored the hearth until they landed on the same stone that Botley had removed moments earlier. With great ease, she withdrew the stone from the wall, as if she had done it a thousand times before. But as her hand slid into the empty space, a loud squeal burst from her lips. Her head jerked around sporadically, searching for the missing keepsake. With one erratic twirling motion, Josephine spun into the chair across from Claire.

"Then with the whirl of the wind and a little bitty spin, everything can go awry."

Once the last word passed through Josephine's lips, she slammed her head down hard on the table and her arms went limp at her sides.

Perplexity plagued Claire's face. Something was clearly wrong with Josephine as she remained motionless. Was she dead?

Claire reached across the table and placed her hand on Josephine's head. "Fräulein, Josephine, are you all right?"

A low growl could be heard from the back of Josephine's throat.

Claire rose quickly from the table and backed away.

"Grrraaahhhhh!" Josephine roared, lifting her head and pointing at Claire.

A gust of wind brushed past her while she stood in the doorway.

"Josephine, stop. Stop it," Botley said in a soothing tone. Again, Josephine slammed her head back down on the table, but this time she did it several times in a row.

"Stop! Stop it!" Botley wrapped his arms tightly around her.

"What is wrong with her?" Claire asked, horrified.

"She has always been this way," Botley said, stroking Josephine's hair in a calming manner.

He looked up at the ceiling mumbling a little prayer under his breath. From what little Claire could see, Josephine's eyes rolled back until they finally closed and her body went limp in the old butler's arms.

Botley kissed her on the forehead. "Oh, dear girl," he whispered and then laid Josephine gently down so her head was resting on the table.

Slowly, he made his way over to the door where Claire was still standing.

"What are you going to do with her?" Claire asked.

"Leave her here to rest."

"Leave her? That does not seem proper. Should you not take her to her room?"

"If there is anything I know after working in this house for several years, it is that it does not run 'properly.' The best thing for Josephine is to just let her rest wherever she is. Now, Mademoiselle Du Bois, we should leave for the Countess' study. I believe she wanted to see you by nine."

"I have one very important stop to make before I go see the Countess De Leon."

"She does not have much patience for dawdling."

"As you just said, Herr Botley, this house does not run properly. I do believe the Countess has waited all this time for me to arrive. She can wait a little longer, I think."

Botley's brow furrowed at her words, but then he motioned to the doorway. "Please, lead the way."

Chapter 5
"Whirlwind Adventures"

Botley held the door open so Claire could step out into the secret garden. The fresh scent of flowers hung in the warm August air and the sun caught sporadic glimpses of the brilliance and color trapped within the inner walls of the house.

Claire's mouth opened in wonderment. She found herself looking in every direction at the splendor of this private Utopia that she was privy to enter.

"This is where I shall leave you, Mademoiselle."

"But why? It is so wonderful out here. How can you not want to stay?" Claire pleaded with him.

"I have my suspicions on why you came out here in the first place. I think it best to leave you to your exploring," said Botley, light-heartedly. "Besides, I need to let the Countess know that you will be delayed."

Claire looked at him scornfully. "If you must. Please let her know that I will not be far behind you."

"Of course, Mademoiselle." He bowed ceremoniously, and then exited back into the house.

Gossip

Claire did not linger. She turned down the small dirt and grass mixed path and allowed her body to move freely through the flowers.

She hadn't walked but a few seconds before she saw Genevieve sitting on a bench under a tree, reading.

"Fräulein Genevieve," Claire said softly so as to not startle her.

Genevieve looked up with some kind of unspoken cheerlessness in her eyes, nothing like the enthusiastic woman that had snuck into Claire's room the night before.

Claire sat down next to her. Genevieve allowed the book to close and rested her hands comfortably on the cover.

"What is wrong?"

Genevieve's eyes shut and her face contorted into her thoughts.

"I fell in love at a young age," Genevieve said at last. "It was not the prince, as the gossip goes, but instead a farm boy to whom I gave my heart."

"I have not noticed any men of your age on the estate. Is he still here?"

Genevieve quietly shook her head.

"Then how-"

Genevieve's sharp eyes darted to Claire, silencing her.

"Children love to allow their minds to run away with them. That is what is so wonderful about children; they're so oblivious to the harsh realities of this world. In my ventures out to the woods, I found myself being a daring swordswoman."

"Honestly?" Claire chuckled, not being able to comprehend this of Genevieve.

"Do not laugh. I was quite good."

"I am sure you were," Claire said, bemused.

"I was alone in the woods one afternoon. A bunch of trees had fallen and how I loved to climb on them. I was a great swordswoman," she said again emphatically, 'who dueled evil creatures lurking around. Then, from nowhere, a bunch of birds were startled and flew past me. I fell from a great height and when I landed I could hear my ankle crack. All I could feel was sharp pain shooting up my leg."

"What did you do?"

"Well, I cried for a while."

"No prince came to save you?"

"No. No prince, but instead the farm boy who just so happened to be collecting firewood. I yelled out to him to come help me, but for a long moment he did not move. He just stared at me with a contented smile on his face. I was not sure where the amusement was coming from considering that I was in a great deal of pain.

"Before long, he made his way to me. He was strong enough that he could lift me as if I weighed nothing. Though it hurt, I bore it. He was not a gentle sort of person. When he carried me, for what felt like days, my body was jostled around a lot in his loose grip."

"I guess you were used to being handled with more care," Claire interjected.

Genevieve snickered at the remark but then followed it with, "I suppose you are right. Though, I also think he took some pleasure in saving an unfortunate little rich girl who hurt herself."

"Perhaps. It was a moment of servitude for him. I assume you made it out of the woods?"

"Yes, the trees started to thin, and I found myself on the edge of a vineyard. Its magnificence was indescribable."

"Please try," Claire said, leaning forward with great interest.

"Magical," escaped her lips. Genevieve looked up at her with an embarrassed smile. "I sound like a giddy school girl, but it was magical."

She put her hand on her chest as if she were trying to catch her breath, and then smiled more brightly than before, lost in the beautiful memory.

"He carried me through the endless sea of grape vines. I would guess we made it a good distance across the vineyard when my weight became too much to bear and he gently sat me down on the ground.

"'Why have we stopped?' I inquired. My foot had been throbbing badly and I just wanted to see the doctor. Much to my surprise the boy pulled out a little knife, leaned over, and cut off a chunk of the thin vine.

"I thought he had lost his mind, but then he stretched out the vine and tightly wrapped it around my ankle. 'I can tell you are in great pain. This should help.'

"That was the first time I had heard his gentle voice. Even now, I can hear it clearly as if he had spoken to me yesterday."

"I can see why you are taken with him. He seems quite charming, even if he is not a prince," Claire said, sounding as if she too were falling in love with him.

"We did not travel much farther before the top of a thatched roof popped into sight. In an instant, we were standing at the other end of the vineyard. I felt relieved initially, but then when he put me down on the ground, he disappeared around the side of the barn."

"He left you?"

"I called after him for several minutes but he was gone. So, I sat alone with sharp pain and the groans as my only company. It was quite some time before the old farmer came running from behind the barn. He scooped me up and took me into the care of his home and quickly sent someone to fetch my mother."

"At least you were all right and your mother was on her way," Claire interjected.

"Again, you would think so. When my mother's carriage arrived, I wanted nothing more than to be in the comfort of my own bed while I recovered. It was not until my mother thanked him that everything seemed ... strange."

"How do you mean?"

"Well the farmer said that it was not he we should be thanking but instead Michael, the young boy, with whom our gratitude should be placed. For it was he who ran through several vine fields to find the farmer and sent him back to me.

"I was aghast. After thinking he had left me for dead, I was shocked to find that he was the reason the farmer was rushing to me the first place.

"My mother offered the farmer a monetary thank you, but he refused to take such a gift. Instead, he helped us into our carriage and we were on our way home. I remember looking out at the field that I had spent a good length of time traveling through only hours before. Just as the field was almost out of sight, I saw him. The farm boy was standing on the edge of the field with a huge smile; he slid his cap off and bowed to me. I could feel my heart racing and became slightly faint. At the time, it was an odd feeling but I realize now that it was love."

"To find it at such a young age is a blessing," Claire said sincerely, but Genevieve didn't even crack a smile. "All right, then what happened?"

"That night I replayed the events from the day over and over again through my mind. Several nights I snuck out of the house and tried to get back to that farm. And a few times I was quite successful, but I was only with Michael for a short time before my mother found me again and took me home. She did not approve of him nor his lowly status.

"The rich must marry the rich. That is how it has always been," Claire affirmed.

Genevieve looked up toward the second story of the house. "Mother thought so too. She finally went to the farmer and paid to get rid of Michael, so he could no longer distract me."

With all the seriousness in Genevieve's eyes, Claire could not help but follow her gaze to see what had captured her attention. Her eyes met with the eyes of the Countess De Leon looking down at them from her study window. A scowl was quite present.

After several uncomfortable seconds, the Countess grabbed the drapes and yanked them shut, disappearing back into her study.

"Do not let her bother you, Mademoiselle Du Bois. She is only angry that I am taking you away from her at the moment. You have nothing to fear."

Claire looked back at Genevieve who was now half smiling at her. "I am not afraid. I just wish to hear the rest of your story. How does it end?"

"Mother had the farmer send Michael away. I am sure it took a lot of provoking, maybe even threatening his young life. I cannot say. What I made clear was how devastated I was when he was gone. I thought I would never see him again."

"There is hope in your voice. What has happened since that time?" Claire said, straightforwardly.

"I received this about a year ago," Genevieve said, holding out a piece of cloth with the emblem of the royal court painted on it.

"How do you know the Queen did not send this to you?" asked Claire, studying the fabric closely.

"Because this came with it." She held out a little piece of dried vine.

After Claire was done examining both the vine and the emblem, she handed them back to Genevieve. "Why have you really called me here?"

"I want you to help me find Michael."

Claire gave a crooked smile as if Genevieve were telling an awful joke. "I cannot get out of this house any easier than you can."

"I wish I knew how to find him on my own, but I cannot. And I have been damned here by my stepsister's anger. You have a far better chance crossing her path than I. The only thing that has held me strong these seven long years is the idea of finding Michael again. He could take me far away from this hell I have been living in. Please Claire, you are my only hope."

Claire rose from the bench and stepped away for a moment. Thoughts of her being arrested and thrown into prison came flooding back.

Genevieve paused. "I am sorry. I did not mean to press you on this matter that would put you at great risk. I just want to find Michael and you are the first hope I have had in years."

When Claire turned back to Genevieve and saw her saddened face, she knew Genevieve was not speaking falsely in saying that Claire was her only hope.

"I do not know what I can do, but I will try my best to help you find him," Claire said reluctantly.

Genevieve jumped from her seat and wrapped her arms tightly around Claire's neck, hugging her new friend close. "Thank you! Thank you!"

Claire pulled Genevieve away. "Now, I must go up to see your mother, as she too needs my help."

Genevieve nodded her head in understanding before sitting back down on the bench and opening her book.

Claire started to make her way down the path back to the entrance of the house. When she looked back one last time at Genevieve, there was a grin that went from ear to ear across her face and an unusual glow about her. Claire had an inkling that it had been a long time since Genevieve felt that good about her life.

Chapter 6
"Locked Doors"

Claire found that her feet already knew where they were taking her. Carrying herself up the staircase to the upper hall, and down the long corridor, she found her way to the worn wooden door to the tower.

She cautiously looked both ways down the hall to make sure that this time she was in the clear. When she felt she was safe, she opened the door and plunged through. Without knowing what had happened, Claire collided right into Botley, who was just on the other side.

"Oh, my goodness, Mademoiselle Du Bois. Are you all right?" Botley said, helping her off the floor.

"I believe so," she said, brushing off her dress.

"Still trying to get up to Isabella's room, I see," Botley said, accusingly.

Claire smirked at the snide remark. "It is interesting that you are here . . . again. Pray, tell me, do you live in the tower or do you simply guard it with your life?"

"I do not know what you think you are going to find up there."

Claire looked past Botley, to the spiral stair that lead up to where she longed to go. Out of the corner of her eye, she saw Botley drop a small silver key into his coat pocket. Redirecting her attention back to him, she said, "Please, Herr Botley."

The old butler did not even argue with her before stepping aside and allowing her free access to the stairway. Claire felt weightless as her feet rushed upward until they found themselves in front of another wooden door. The only light cast upon it came from a single little window above the staircase.

From what Claire could see, this door was uniquely different from any other door she had seen in the Countess' house. The wood was of a hard maple and stained a deep red. In the center of the door was a detailed engraving of a pumpkin.

Claire placed her hand down on the heart of the carving and allowed her fingers to sprawl across the intricacies of its craftsmanship.

"Fascinating, is it not?" Botley said, now standing next to her.

"This is it. This is the ever famous pumpkin," Claire declared.

"Count Daughtry traveled all over the world collecting the most auspicious items on his voyages," Botley said with amusement. "I believe he got this door in China."

"Has the pumpkin always been carved into the door?" Claire inquired, still feeling the deep grooves. "Or did he have someone else put it there?"

"That is how he found the door. It seems that pumpkins are seen as a sign of prosperity and fruitfulness in one's life. I guess the Count took some interest in this idea and got this along with a handful of other things for Isabella, so that she might live a prosperous life."

"She is certainly doing that," Claire agreed with the thought.

As her hand ran along the surface of the door it hit something cool to the touch. Taking a closer look, she noticed a large, cast iron door handle with a lock.

"Hmm," resonated on her lips. "Fascinating, indeed."

Claire turned to Botley as if asking permission to go into the room. The old butler pushed down on the handle and shoved the door open.

Inside was nothing like Claire had imagined. A queen-sized bed rested to the right side of the room. It was neither decorated nor fanciful in its design. Next to the bed was a little night table made of the same wood as the bed and just as dull in appearance. A large wardrobe was the only piece of furniture on the opposite side and at the far end rested a small writing desk next to a quaint window.

Claire entered, slowly taking in every aspect of this simple room. When she reached the wardrobe, she tried to open it but it was securely locked. Remembering the key from only moments before, she quickly looked over to Botley for an explanation.

"I am sorry, Mademoiselle. The Countess thought you might make your way up here and did not feel you are ready to see the contents of the wardrobe."

Claire let go of the wardrobe in dismay. She moved over to the writing desk. It had had a lot of use in its years clearly seen with the scratches and nicks in random places. She tried to lift the lid to see the contents inside the desk but it too was locked.

She chuckled to herself. "I now see what you meant about not finding anything up here, Herr Botley."

"I did try to warn you."

"That is only because you will not allow me to be privy to the Queen's things."

"The Countess knows what she is doing. She will let you see Isabella's things when she is ready for you to, not the other way around."

"I see. Well, I did learn one thing by coming up here. There is a lock on that door. That definitely will require an explanation by the Countess."

"You think so?" Botley said with a quizzical brow. He grabbed an iron key that was hanging on the wall right next to the door. The key slid perfectly into the keyhole and when he turned it, Claire could hear the door lock.

She looked at the old butler with question because he had just locked the two of them into the tower.

"The lock was meant to keep people out of the room, not to lock them in," Botley said, and unlocked the door again.

He pushed the door open. "I do believe you have kept the Countess waiting long enough."

"Of course. You are right," Claire agreed. Before she stepped out, she glanced one last time at the room to keep the image fresh in her mind.

* * *

When the two approached the study, the door flew open and the Countess' thin figure filled the doorway.

"I will take her from here, Botley," she snapped.

The old butler bowed his head and dismissed himself.

Disapproval was apparent on the Countess' face. Claire was beginning to grow accustomed to the expression. After several moments of suffering under the harsh glare, Claire was finally permitted to pass as the Countess stepped aside.

The only things that moved were the Countess' eyes, watching her until she was comfortably seated in the chair in front of the large desk.

After a long moment, the Countess closed the study door and slowly made her way over to her seat in front of the desk.

"I know you are curious about this place, and you are curious why I chose you, of all people, to come speak with me in my home."

"Very true on both accounts."

"I promise in time you will have all the answers you seek, but you must stop prying around my house. More importantly, I brought you here to speak with me, not my daughters."

Claire looked at the Countess firmly. "Fräulein Genevieve approached me."

The Countess' eyes closed, much like Genevieve's had earlier, and she said, "My daughter is searching for a dream that has long since been lost. Please do not encourage her grand delusions."

"There is no harm in wishing to have a good piece of your life back," Claire argued.

"Mademoiselle Du Bois, that farm boy was never going to marry my daughter. She needs to realize that she has a certain status in society and she needs to live within its parameters."

"She has found love with Michael. Does that not count for anything?"

Gossip

"Love will not put a roof over her head. Security is what she needs, if she can find it after all this mess. Not love."

Claire pulled out some parchment and a quill, avoiding eye contact with the Countess De Leon.

"I disagree with you, Countess. Love may be the only thing that is going to save Fräulein Genevieve from this 'mess,' as you call it."

Claire allowed her eyes to go up and meet the Countess'. For the first time since being there, it was the Countess that looked away.

"I know where you get that strong will of yours, Mademoiselle Du Bois. So, instead of arguing with you I will simply ask, please do not get involved."

Claire thought for a moment. "I have no intentions of leaving this house, so I am not sure how I could have helped Fräulein Genevieve anyway."

"That is not the promise I wish to hear," the Countess stated coldly.

"I will not go looking for Michael," Claire agreed. "Now, may we get back to the story of you and the Count?"

"Of course. Let me see. Where did I leave off?"

Chapter 7
"The Little Cinder Girl"

"Count Daughtry and I were married after a very short courtship. He was not at all a traditional man, constantly misleading me into believing one thing when in fact he had other things in mind."

"Why did you stay with him then?" Claire inquired. "There were certainly other available men in court I should think."

The Countess De Leon's fingers interlaced one another, clasping together as they rested on her desk.

"He was a pirate in nature, but there was something about his unpredictability that I enjoyed. I never knew what tomorrow would bring, nor did I care . . . He loved to travel. Most of his investments were in trade in foreign lands."

"Did you ever get to go with him on his travels?" Claire asked.

"We went to a few places outside of France, but I could not be sure if he did any trading in them. He seemed to know everyone no matter where we went and I think he just wanted to show me off. He would buy me extravagant gifts, such as large diamond necklaces, so that I would draw even more attention from his peers. I was satisfied knowing that there was someone who wanted to dote on me. He wanted me to feel like a queen."

The Countess broke off and looked away. Claire still scribbled away at the page trying to catch up to the Countess' last thoughts.

"Please, continue."

"We had taken a carriage to Italy. Being a good Catholic woman, I wanted nothing more than to see Rome. Pulling into the streets, the city itself was alive with music and culture. A large theatre festival was going on at the time, and being that Charles revered acting, we attended. The theatres were not like they are here. There is no building to go into with stages that sat apart from the audience. Instead, you walked into what looked like a miniature Coliseum. No lights, no scenery; just the actors and the cement stage under their feet.

"We saw 'The Captives,' by Plautus, I think it was. At the end of the show, we all rose in applause. Then, something very unexpected happened. The lead actor looked right at me. It did not seem like much at the time, but then he came into the crowd, grabbed my hand and dragged me back down to the stage. When I looked back for Count Daughtry, he was gone.

"I was so embarrassed. I could not tell what was going on or why. The actor started to speak to the crowd in Italian. I could not make out a word that he was saying. The next thing I know, I am being paraded around the stage to the whole audience like I am some prize to be won, and to make matters worse, they were cheering loudly.

"Well, I had had quite enough of the foolishness. In a moment, I snatched my hand back from the actor and started to make my way out of the theatre. When I approached the exit, actors appeared out of nowhere and blocked my escape."

"What did you do?" Claire asked, almost breathless. She was leaning forward in her chair, enthralled in the story.

"I turned back to the lead actor who was standing in the center of the stage giving me a devilish smile. His eyes seemed to light up under the long grey strings of hair that covered his face. I did not need to speak Italian to know that he was up to no good."

"Were you scared?"

"Certainly not. I just crossed to the other side of the stage to exit from there."

"Did you succeed?"

"Not exactly, no. Two more actors popped up and blocked my escape. There was no telling if I was ever going to get out of there. Then I heard, 'Desiree'. When I turned, Count Daughtry was standing center stage next to the lead actor."

"What did you do?"

"What could I do? I walked over to him. The crowd started chanting. Again, I could not understand a single word, but I could feel from the knots in my stomach that whatever was happening was going to be extraordinary.

"When I drew closer to him, he took my hand in his and he knelt. 'Desiree De Leon,' he said to me. 'I want nothing more in my life than for you to be my wife.'"

"You said yes, right?" Claire's voice held so much excitement that it was starting to get hard to sit.

"I believe I said something like, 'pardon me?' I was not sure I had heard him correctly. He turned to the crowd and said something in Italian that got them to be silent."

Claire looked up at her, eyes calculated. "You are saying that Count Daughtry spoke Italian?"

"I did not know it myself until that moment, but yes. Again, the man was an absolute bafflement to me, but I endured him."

"Please, I want to know more about the proposal," Claire interjected, not wanting to stray too far from the story.

"He looked back at me with his deep brown eyes and said, 'Desiree, please, I know there is a lot to me you do not know or I about you. But think of it, we could spend the rest of our lives listening to each other's stories and even making new ones of our own.'"

"I can see what intrigued you so," said Claire with a little chuckle.

The Countess De Leon's face flushed a little and she half-smiled. Her eyes gazed at Claire for a moment but then drifted back into the memory.

"What was your reply to him?"

"I believe 'yes' finally escaped my lips, because we were married shortly after."

"Did your family attend?"

"I wanted my girls to be there but to return to France and try to make all the proper arrangements would have taken months. Count Daughtry was too impulsive for that."

"I will assume then that you were married in Rome?"

"Yes. It was a simple affair, and by simple I mean all of the theatre festival celebrated with us. Another little detail I did not know about the Count was that he played a big hand in financing some of the theatre troupes there in Rome."

To see the look of annoyance on the Countess' face, it took Claire everything shy of covering her mouth to not chuckle.

"Sure, you might think it funny, but not knowing things about your husband, such as his affairs in other countries or how many languages he might speak, can make a woman grow weary."

"But think of it Countess, what wonders that were left for you to discover."

The Countess pursed her lips. "The only wonder that I had to discover upon our return to France was that of his daughter, Isabella."

"So you did not know of her until after you were married?'

"I knew he had been married before but there was no mention of his daughter."

"What was it like when you first met her?"

"Peculiar. My two daughters and I packed up our belongings and traveled to his estate in which you now find yourself. As we approached, I could not believe how magnificent the whole idea was to me."

"What do you mean?"

"I had just married a handsome man with a large estate. What else could any woman of my age and situation want for herself and her family?"

"However?"

"However," said the Countess, picking up right off of the cue. "The whole dream was shattered when the carriage door opened and I first laid eyes on his little girl who was covered from head to toe in dirt."

"Dirt?"

"Well, chimney ash, to be correct."

"What did you say?"

"What any woman would say in that situation. 'Why did you not tell me you had a daughter?'"

"And he said?"

"'I did not want to spoil the surprise.'"

"That cannot be what he said."

"Ah . . . but it was. Nothing could change the scenario so I merely went over to shake hands with the girl, but she crossed her arms and turned away from me immediately. I tell you, she smelled as if she had been sleeping with the pigs. Her hair was all matted down with twigs and dirt embedded into it, and her clothes and face were stained in ash.

"Count Daughtry could tell my disapproval of her appearance and said 'She is a spirited girl who is very playful.' He looked down at Isabella and patted her dress. A wall of cinder ash flew into the air. I took a step back to avoid inhaling it. As the dust settled, Count Daughtry threw on a dashing smile and simply said, 'She likes to read near the fireplace. Sometimes she gets a little too close.'

"'I can see that,' I said, covering my nose to block the stench."

Claire began to bite her lower lip before she said, "Did you think her pretty?"

The Countess' eyes shot up to meet Claire's. "What do you mean?"

Claire looked down at the paper covered in notes in front of her. After rereading the last line about the cinder-covered girl she looked back up at the Countess. "Did you find her to be more attractive then either one of your daughters?"

"Did I not just tell you how her appearance repulsed me?"

"Yes, but you could have been equally as repulsed had she been a beautiful young lady."

The Countess' fingers began to tap the desk while an annoyed scowl crossed her face.

"I know that is what the town's people think. They think that little Isabella was a threat to me and my daughters so I hid her away."

"Well, that is how it came to me in Germany."

"Let me assure you that the gossip gets worse."

"Countess-"

"They can be down right cruel at times."

"Countess, I am not interested in what gossip is going around the Queen's court. I am more interested in hearing what you have to tell me. Please, I would like you to continue."

The Countess' raised eyebrow relaxed and she let out a little huff. "Charles was a whirlwind adventure that, I am sad to say, I did not get to have for very long."

"Were you with him when he . . ."

"Died?" the Countess grunted.

"Yes," Claire whispered, looking a little ashamed she asked the question.

"That morning will be captured in my mind forever. That was the morning that everything changed. And I do mean everything.

"We had only been married a few months and I was still adapting to my new environment. Charles had received word that there was some trouble with two of his ships docking in Barcelona. He immediately packed a bag and hopped on his horse.

"'Is there no one else who can handle this affair?' I pleaded with him. But he would not listen to me. In hindsight, I knew he would be going as soon as the messenger dropped off the letter. He was always headstrong and had to handle his own business."

"How much time was it before he left?"

"No more than a day, I believe. I could tell that the matter stressed him. That was the first time I knew of that something in his business had gone awry. After it all happened . . . I remember the only sound that drowned out my own tears that night was the sound of Isabella's."

"I would guess she was upset," Claire admitted.

"I would say more so. She was very attached to Charles. I am sure she felt like she was living with complete strangers, not having much time to get to know either my daughters or me."

"A few months is not a lot of time."

"You are right." The Countess sat back in her chair and took a deep breath.

"The whole household was outside to see Charles off that morning. He said his fond farewells, mounted his horse, and started on his way.

"I could feel my stomach start to turn and my emotions getting the best of me. I could not bear to see him go, nor could I let the children see me in this state. So, I hurried back into the house, not wanting to watch him disappear into the distance.

"I could hear Isabella say something about tradition and him waving back at us, but I could not wait for that. The tears were already starting to overcome me. I had made it no more than two steps inside the door when I heard a shriek. When I turned back, Charles was lying on the ground.

"Isabella made it to him before I did. We watched him struggle to breathe. His eyes started on me, but then moved to her. 'I love you always,' he said. And with that, he died."

The room went silent after the Countess' last words. Claire saw the tears forming once more in the Countess' eyes while she relived the horrific event.

The Countess slid a handkerchief from her pocket to dab her eyes, then rested her hands in her lap comfortably.

"I try very hard to forget that day, but, like I said, it is a memory that will forever be trapped in my mind. For I believe that was the day that my whole life would make a turn for the worst."

"Why do you say that?" Claire asked.

"I told you everything changed that day. Maybe I should be more specific; Isabella changed that day. After Charles stopped breathing, both Isabella and I wept over his body. I could not imagine what was going through her mind. She never knew her mother and now her father was gone. I reached out to embrace her when she looked up at me with the most awful glare. 'You did this to him, I know you did. I will never forgive you! Never!'"

"What did you say?"

"What could I say? She was a young and impressionable child. I do not know why she thought that I would ever want to harm Charles."

"It really sounds like you went through quite an ordeal."

"Mademoiselle Du Bois, Charles' death was only just the beginning."

Chapter 8
"Squeaky Clean"

"Tell me about Isabella's cleaning habits," Claire asked candidly. "I know that many people say you forced her to clean the house, but I get the sense that it did not happen like that at all."

"Obviously the town's people have never been in my home to know that this house is fully staffed with servants to do all of the chores. Why on earth would I need Isabella doing them?"

"You tell me."

A wry expression captured the Countess' hard face. "She started with the floors. At least that is the first thing that I can remember. I woke up early the morning after Charles' funeral. I could not sleep, so I thought it best to go get a small bite to eat. Maybe it would calm my nerves.

"I took a step out into the hall, and without knowing what was going on, I felt my feet slid out from underneath me. I hit the floor hard and lay there for a few minutes. I could feel cool water soaking into my nightgown and all I could ask myself was, 'Why is there a puddle of water on the floor?'

"When my thoughts began to refocus, I could hear a scrubbing sound coming from down the hall. Surely it was too early for any of the servants to be up. I lifted my candlestick to identify the strange noise and there was Isabella, on her hands and knees, scouring the floor.

"I asked her what she thought she was doing out of bed in the middle of the night, but she did not acknowledge me. She just continued to scrub the floor in silence."

"Did you attempt to stop her?"

"I knelt down in front of her and placed my hand on the brush."

"And?"

Claire noticed the Countess shudder.

"She looked at me."

"That is all? She looked at you?"

"You make it sound so trivial, but this was no ordinary glare. It was filled with hate and pain; to the point that I thought she might attack me. I could even swear I heard a low growl in the back of her throat. I was frightened, and I do not say that lightly, Mademoiselle Du Bois."

The Countess shifted her weight in her chair, looking uncomfortable. Still, she continued.

"In all my travels and of all the sordid people I have met, I can not recall a person I was more afraid of than Isabella in that moment."

"What did you do?"

"I backed away from her and let her continue cleaning the floor."

"Did you stay with her?"

"I thought about it, but no. I was uncomfortable and found myself wanting very much to hide behind a locked door."

"She was only a confused little girl. There is no way she was going to hurt you."

The Countess shifted again in her chair until she sat up perfectly straight, and glowered at Claire.

"A little puppy may seem harmless, but if you hit it enough times, it will eventually bite you back."

"But you were not hitting her. You were trying to care for her."

"You and I know that, but she on the other hand . . ."

"And this is how the gossip began?" Claire concluded.

The Countess De Leon dropped her head in acknowledgement.

Claire sat back in her chair, looking the Countess over more carefully. It wasn't just her words that suggested the trepidation she felt toward Isabella, but also her body language and the constant shifting in her seat. That little girl clearly struck fear into this strong woman.

"Tell me more about her cleaning."

"The next morning, I woke believing I had dreamt the whole thing up. However, when I went to get out of bed, I found a bruise on my leg from when I fell and my back was stiff.

"I apprehensively went over to my door and peeked into the hall. Much to my relief, it was empty."

"At least you know she did not stay out there all night."

"Just because she was not present does not mean that she had not been there for some time over the course of the evening."

"Was that all she did? Clean the floors?"

"Not even close. That morning I went down to breakfast where Genevieve had already started eating her eggs, ham, and fruit. It was a pleasant surprise to see it already made and on the table for us. But when I went down to compliment Cook for being ahead of our usual morning schedule, he was in the kitchen waiting for the bread to finish baking so he could start the eggs.

"'Do you not think we have already had enough for breakfast? I think one course is plenty.' He looked at me as if I were speaking a foreign language.

"'This is the first course, Mam.' he said shortly. 'Then how?' I started but decided not to finish the thought. Instead, I told him to think forward to lunch because we had already eaten. He grumbled a bit but did as I asked."

"Cleaning to cooking. That is certainly kind of her. Though, it does pose the question of why she would be so nice if she did not care for you."

"Honestly, I wish I could tell you. My guess is she read it out of some book. Evil witch making the poor servant girl do all the work."

Claire could tell the Countess was recounting the fairy tale book almost scene by scene. Still, she left the book in her satchel for the time being.

"The next night, I woke up to a strange 'thumping' sound. Again, I moved cautiously to my door and poked my head out. This time she had taken a large broomstick and was beating all the dust from the tapestries and the curtains.

"The moonlight caught the thick cloud of dust that hovered around her. I was curious if she was going to clean the upper half of the curtains or only what she could reach."

"I bet she cleaned the whole thing," Claire interjected.

"She did. She pulled out a chair. She must have dragged it from the study, and climbed on top of it to start hitting the top part of the curtain."

"Smart."

"Odd does not necessarily mean ignorant," the Countess scoffed.

"Why do you think she only cleaned at night?"

"I suppose it was so no one would stop her. At least that is the best guess I have. But that was only at the beginning."

"So, she did start cleaning during the day."

"About a week or two later, it became a daily routine. She would start with washing her clothes down by the river."

"By herself?"

"Most of the time. On a rare occasion, Josephine joined her."

"Hmm," Claire hummed while starting to put the pieces together in her mind.

"She liked nature, so who was I to stop her from going out there?"

"Go on."

"After washing clothes, she would polish the silver with Cook. He did not seem to understand it but never turned down the extra help she gave him. Then, she would make her way out to the stables. I assume it was to clean the stalls and feed the horses. Botley would tend to join her on this chore. I think they snuck carrots out to Count Daughtry's horse, but also, it allowed Isabella alone time to speak with someone she could trust.

In the late afternoon, she would take a bucket and scrub down the floors in the main entrance hall. After several hours of work, she would eat a quiet supper by the fire while reading a book, and then head up to bed."

"That sounds like a pretty full day."

"It was indeed, and she did it every day."

"Interesting."

"The only days she became difficult about it were days that it rained. Of course, our shoes tended to be covered with mud from walking in town or on the drive. When we walked into the house, I made sure the girls cleaned their feet as best they could. However, if a single drop of mud hit the ground, Isabella would shriek loudly just before going to retrieve a bucket of water and then scrub the entire floor clean ... again."

"Whoa. That is strange."

"She would not even look at the floor but glared at us instead, mumbling things under her breath."

"Trying to look on the bright side, at least your house was always clean."

The Countess dropped her hands on her desk and looked at Claire in disbelief.

"Honestly, the amount of criticism I have received for that girl's odd cleaning behavior is far from the worth of having a clean house."

"I suppose you are right. I am sorry you have had to endure not only Isabella but the false accusations that came with her cleaning," Claire said apologetically.

"The amount of cleaning that girl did was almost unattainable by one individual. One morning I woke up and the first thing I noticed was the amount of light coming through the windows. They were spotless, and all the drapes had been beaten clean and drawn back. The next thing I noticed was the statues had all been thoroughly dusted and polished and the floor had been wiped clean."

"How could it be done?"

"I wish I knew. The best servant I ever had could not have put as much care and precision into all that Isabella accomplished in that one night."

"Do you think someone helped her?"

"She might tell you that her Fairy Godmother did."

"You and I already know that is not true." Claire's hand delved into her satchel and produced the small book.

Pulling it out, Claire tossed it onto the desk. "Why not help me get acquainted with her?" she said assertively.

The Countess stared at the book momentarily, then flipped open the cover. Skimming through the pages, she finally stopped on the picture of the Fairy Queen.

Claire tried to get a closer look at the majestic creature that floated across the whole page, but the Countess rested her hand perfectly so that most of the image was hidden from view.

"What does the fairy godmother mean to you?" asked Claire sincerely.

"I would think the person who gave you this book would have told you its significance to me," the Countess said accusingly.

Just as the words escaped from the Countess' lips, there was a light knock at the door.

"Come in," said the Countess.

Botley came in and bowed. "I apologize for the intrusion," he said. Claire turned to look at him but the Countess did not.

He continued. "Mademoiselle Du Bois, your friend, Monsieur Krouse..."

"Is he here?"

"He is."

"All right. Tell him I will be right down for dinner. I just need to finish with the Countess."

Botley didn't flinch.

"Well?" the Countess hissed. Botley nodded his head solemnly.

Slightly confused as to what was going on, Claire turned back to catch the Countess pondering something.

"What is it?"

The Countess redirected her eyes to Botley. "Where is he?"

"I put him in the guest room next to Mademoiselle Du Bois, just as you requested, Madam."

The Countess stood up and hastily exited the study. Claire looked back to Botley perplexed.

"Is she angry that my friend has come?'

"No. More like, she predicted the way in which he would arrive."

"And?" Claire barked.

"And, she was correct."

Chapter 9
"Integral Part"

Claire lost her breath as she barreled down the hall toward the open door to Victor's bedchamber.

When she entered his room, Claire's legs almost buckled underneath her. Lying in the bed, unconscious, was her dear friend, Victor. A nurse tended to the gash over his brow and it was hard to miss the multiple scrapes and bruises that covered his arms.

"What happened?" Claire gasped.

The Countess, who was standing on the far side of the bed, looked up at Claire, unmoved.

"The Queen," she said simply.

Claire moved to the vacant seat next to the bed and scooped Victor's hand into hers.

"Victor?" Claire whispered, but there was no response. Looking over his wounds, she caught the mix of small pebbles and blood strewn through his long, dark hair.

Grabbing a wet cloth from the basin on the nightstand, she dabbed the cut on his brow line. Fury and terror swarmed through her, causing her whole body to tremble.

The nurse took the cloth from Claire's hand. "Mademoiselle, I will take good care of him, I promise."

Claire relinquished the cloth in her hand, and then shot a knowing look at the Countess. The Countess' face was unsympathetic.

Not wanting to linger any longer, Claire made her way out to the hallway. She could feel that the Countess was on her heel. When she heard the door close to Victor's room, she spun around.

"You knew this was going to happen?"

"I had my suspicions," stated the Countess, matter-of-factly.

"Why did you not warn us? Why did you not let me know how much danger I would be in by coming here?"

"I needed you to come." the Countess said sternly. "You are my only chance."

"At what?!" Claire screamed, losing her composure.

The Countess walked right up to Claire so that their faces were inches apart. "A normal life! Look, I am sorry for your friend's misfortune, but my daughters and I have suffered the same consequences day in and day out for seven years!"

Claire didn't even blink to cut the tension. Instead, she started for her own bedchamber door.

"I will be returning home once Victor is well enough to travel."

"Why did you come here, Claire?" the Countess shouted after her. "If my memory serves me correctly, you want to find your father."

At this, Claire's hand loosened on the door handle until her arm fell limp at her side. The Countess had her, and what was worse is that she knew it. Claire's jaw tightened from her clenched teeth and her mind raced at the Countess' words.

"It is an absolute shame that I know his identity," the Countess said, more poised, while moving toward her.

"How could you know that?" Claire said, stunned.

"Last night you said you did not want to stay with me because you had other business in town. Personal business. You wanted to snoop around to find out where your mother came from and hopefully find out the identity of your father."

Claire turned to the Countess, who was now a few feet away from her.

"Is it wrong to want to know my father?"

"Only if it will get you into more trouble than you are already in."

Stepping closer to the Countess, Claire said, "Will it really?"

The Countess looked down at the ground seriously, and nodded.

"Then tell me. Why all the secrecy?"

"If I tell you how I know that you are the Baron Dupree or the identity of your father, you might not stay to finish listening to my story."

"But I will," Claire pleaded.

The Countess shook her head. "I cannot take that risk. I am sorry, you are too integral to what is going on here."

"What do you mean?"

"You still do not understand. I am a traitor by every word I say to you that contradicts the Queen's story. It is imperative that we finish before ..."

"Before?" Claire barked, losing patience.

The Countess huffed. "Before I must go."

"Is all this worth it?"

"It will be."

"I hope for all our sakes that you know what you are doing."

The Countess looked unflinchingly into Claire's eyes. "I do."

"All right then. Night is upon us. I think I will take my dinner alone. We can continue tomorrow morning, after I spend a little time with Victor to make sure he is all right."

"Fine," the Countess said shortly.

The two women stared at each other for a long moment. Then Claire broke away and went into her bedchamber.

* * *

Other than the crackling in the fireplace, the dining room was tranquil. The Countess kept her promise and allowed Claire to eat alone. She sat quietly lost in her thoughts when—"Whoosh!" sounded from behind the curtains, breaking Claire's concentration.

Looking down the row of windows, all the drapes had been pulled and rested comfortably against the wall except for one. The last curtain, furthest from where she sat, was protruding from the wall with something moving behind it.

At first Claire looked up and down the hidden object, and then, "Whoosh!" sounded again.

"Josephine?" Claire said softly.

A small spatter of giggles shot from behind the curtain. Josephine poked her head out and looked at her through her stringy, black hair. After a moment, she went back into hiding.

Claire rose from her seat and took slow, calculated steps along the row of windows until she reached the curtain Josephine was standing behind.

"Whoosh!" sounded again.

When Claire reached out and pulled the fabric back, Josephine let out a high pitched squeal that melted into laughter. All of a sudden her body went stiff as a board and she fell flat on the ground.

Claire quickly knelt beside her, "Josephine?"

"Falling down, falling down, if you get caught you will be falling down." Josephine sang. Pushing her feet against the floor, she rotated her body in circles while she remained on her back.

Claire moved out of her way to avoid getting stepped on.

All of a sudden Josephine sat up straight and looked at her. "Green!"

"Green?" Claire repeated.

"Green is the color all love in their sight, but not she who hates it with all her spite."

"Who could hate a color?"

"Green is the color all love in their sight, but not she who hates it with all her spite."

Josephine raised her hand high in the air and like a fallen bird she allowed it to spin and whirl until it landed in her pocket. Then like a most prized possession, she pulled out a large emerald ring and held it out to Claire.

Leaning closer to get a better look, she saw that the stone was flawless. The five-karat emerald was surrounded by four tiny diamonds and locked in place by a sterling silver band. It easily took up a fourth of Josephine's palm.

Claire reached out to take it from her but Josephine snatched her hand back close to her body, hiding it.

"Why did you want to show this to me?" Claire asked, more to herself than Josephine.

A little tune accompanied the answer. "Green is the hated color by she who did not love the owner of thee."

This time, Josephine held her hand out and plopped the ring down into Claire's hand. Before Claire could say anything to her, Josephine curled up in a ball and started rocking back and forth.

"How strange you are," Claire said. "By the sound of things you might have made good friends with Isabella."

"She did."

Claire stood up quickly and turned to see Botley standing by the doorway.

"Herr Botley. You really must stop sneaking up on me like this," Claire said with a light chuckle.

While in the moment of humor, Claire quietly pocketed the emerald ring so the old butler couldn't see it.

Botley moved toward Josephine, who was now lying still on the floor.

Claire looked back down at the frozen girl. "You said that she and Isabella were friends?"

"Yes," Botley said, struggling to get Josephine to sit up. "The best of friends, in fact."

"What that must have been like, I wonder?"

Botley stopped for a moment. "I think it was the best thing to happen for both of them. They kept each other company despite their oddities."

"Then what happened?"

"Isabella met Prince Fabian and she is now living happily ever after."

"Ah," Claire said with understanding.

"What was Josephine doing in here anyway?" Botley asked.

"She was hiding behind the curtain."

"Playing hide and seek with you? Did she tell you anything?" the old butler inquired.

"Nothing that made any sense. Why?"

"She does not play hide and seek with anyone but me. You must be special to her."

Claire flushed crimson.

Botley smiled in his genuinely nice way and said, "I cannot speak for anyone else in the house, but I think you are a right fine lady, Mademoiselle Du Bois. After all, you are putting yourself in harm's way to be here. I know the Countess appreciates it, even if she does not tell you so herself."

"Thank you," she said.

Botley finally got Josephine to her feet. "Now if you will excuse me, I must get her to bed."

"Of course. Have a good night."

"You as well," said Botley, before helping Josephine out of the dining room.

Claire's eyes clung to the entrance a moment longer. Once she was sure she was alone again, she pulled the emerald ring out of her pocket and held it close to her eyes so she could examine it.

A humming tune started in the back of her throat until it finally made its way to her lips. "Green is the color all love in their sight, but not she who hates it with all her spite."

Chapter 10

"Victor Krouse"

Dawn had not yet broken when a creaking sound stirred Claire. Her eyes felt heavy and not wanting to open, but the repetitive creaking sound forced her to wake.

When her eyes fluttered open, she saw Victor gliding back and forth in the rocking chair next to her bed. His eyes were closed with his hands folded over his chest. He had certainly been up long enough to have already gotten dressed.

"Victor!" Claire squealed enthusiastically and sat up in the bed.

Victor's eyes popped open and a gentle smile set in.

"I have no idea what kind of mess you have gotten us into this time, Claire Du Bois, but it seems very exciting," Victor said in amusement.

Claire hopped out of bed and embraced Victor so quickly that she knocked the air out of him.

"I am glad to see you too," said Victor.

"I was so worried about you! Was it the Queen who did this to you?"

"Indirectly, I suppose. The royal guard passed me on the road here. They wanted to know what business I had with the Countess De Leon. I told them that I did not know."

"So they beat you?" gasped Claire.

"They did not care for that as an answer. That, and..."

"And?"

Victor looked away mischievously, whistling a merry tune. Claire pinched his arm tightly between her fingers.

"Victor Krouse!"

"All right! All right," Victor surrendered. "I told one of the guards that his horse's butt had a better chance of getting a girl than he did."

"Victor!" Claire groaned.

"He only got a couple of shots on me before the Captain, who had been traveling separately, passed by. He ordered them to release me immediately."

Claire sat back down on her bed, shaking her head as images of Victor's night played out in her mind.

"Why must you always stir up trouble?"

"It just comes naturally, I suppose."

Claire was not impressed with the charming smile that accompanied his tale.

"Do you want to tell me why we are here?" Victor asked. "I can tell it cannot be good between my rendezvous with the royal guard and you biting your lower lip."

Claire instantly relaxed her lip from under her teeth after his remark.

"The Countess is holding us captive here so she can tell me about her encounters with Queen Isabella."

Victor stared blankly at her.

"It would seem as if the Queen has fabricated her story about her childhood."

"Do you believe that?" Victor asked, trying to catch up with all that Claire has gone through in a day.

"I believe she thinks it is true."

"That is not what I asked." Victor argued.

He tried to sit next to Claire on the bed but she immediately got up and moved over to the window. The sun was now lighting up the room more fully and the circles under Claire's eyes were pronounced.

"She knows about Baron Dupree."

An awkward moment of silence passed before Victor said, "All right."

"And she knows who my father is."

Victor's face dropped. "I see."

Rising from the bed, Victor joined her by the window and placed a caring hand on Claire's shoulder.

"I believe that it is important, not only for our safety but the Countess' as well, that I stay and listen to what she has to tell me," said Claire.

"Agreed."

"But . . ." Claire turned to him. "I want you to return back to Stuttgart. It is far too dangerous for you to stay here. I already know too much, but you can go."

"And leave you to have fun here without me? Nonsense."

Claire's eyes started to water. She looked away, embarrassed. Victor put both his hands onto her shoulders and held her at arm's length.

"Claire, as always, you are overreacting. I am not going to abandon you just because I got a little bump on the head."

Overwhelmed by his kindness and friendship, Claire could feel her arms embracing him with thanks.

Victor dried the tears from Claire's face, finishing it with a kiss on the forehead.

"Why do you not change and I will wait for you in the hall?"

Claire nodded in agreement as she took over wiping her tears away. She watched Victor make his way to the door when she said, "Thank you."

Victor glanced back at her with his charming smile. "For what?"

Before she could answer him, he started whistling loudly again and slipped out the door.

* * *

Botley greeted Claire with a courteous bow when she opened her bedchamber door.

"Oh," she said. Disappointment crossed her face as she looked around for Victor.

"Good morning, Mademoiselle Du Bois."

"Herr Botley. How do you find yourself this morning?"

"I am well, thank you," replied Botley.

Now taking a full step into the hall, Claire didn't even look at the old butler but instead scanned the halls wondering if she simply missed seeing Victor. He was such a prankster and never took anything seriously.

"Excuse me for saying so, but you seem distracted this morning," said Botley, with inquisitiveness.

"Have you seen my friend this morning? We were supposed to go down to breakfast together."

"Monsieur Krouse already went down."

Claire shook her head in disbelief. "If I know anything about Victor Krouse it is that nothing gets in the way of his stomach," she said light-heartedly.

"That might be true," Botley agreed. "However, I also told him you are having breakfast with the Countess in her study. She wanted to meet with you as soon as you woke."

Claire's amusement faded. "I am sure she did. To apologize, I hope."

Botley shrugged his shoulders. Claire knew that even if Botley had known why the Countess wanted to meet so early, he would not divulge that information to her.

"Well, lead on then, Herr Botley. We must not keep her waiting," she said, gesturing down the hall. Botley turned and began walking with Claire alongside him.

"I understand that you are in close connection with the famous author Baron Dupree. I am quite an admirer of his work," Botley said.

"I am sure he would be glad to know that he has admirers in France."

"I am sure that the Baron has admirers that extend farther than that. It would mean a great deal to me if you told him how much his stories have impacted my life."

"It would be my pleasure," Claire said, sincerely. "I am sure he would love to sit and chat with a man such as yourself, Herr Botley. It seems as if you, too, have many secret stories to tell."

"Many secrets, none of which I wish to tell."

"Not even ones about the Queen?" Claire said curiously.

"Perhaps."

"Would you at least tell me what she was like?"

"A dreamer, mostly," recalled the old butler.

"Every girl dreams."

Claire looked over at Botley to gauge his expression, because his tone led her to believe that it wasn't a good thing.

Gossip

Claire continued, "After all the Queen endured, I would think there would be nothing wrong with being a dreamer."

"She started to lose touch with reality," he admitted in dismay. "Once, she found a tattered old dress that belonged to her mother. Though it was twice her size, she wore it everywhere, pretending to be that peasant girl from her book. At first it was harmless, but once the Countess arrived, everything changed."

Claire stopped, and turned to face Botley. "Why do you think that was?"

Botley looked down at the floor, seeming to struggle to find words. "I think the Count remarrying was too much for Isabella. After all, who could possibly stand in her mother's shoes?"

"A witch that casted a spell," Claire said, putting the pieces together.

"Precisely," Botley affirmed before turning down the next hall.

"What about her cleaning habits?" she inquired.

"When the Count died, Isabella started behaving strangely. She would wake up early in the morning and go down to the river to fetch a bucket of water. With a bar of soap and a scrub brush, she would scour the floors, starting in the entrance hall and working her way upstairs."

"Did she really do that every day?"

"Like clockwork."

"It is nice to know the Countess was telling me the truth."

"Maybe I should not be saying this," Botley said, coming to a full stop. "But I do hope you realize that the Countess has nothing to gain from telling you lies. I know she is a stern woman, but she has lived through worse than most care to endeavor in a lifetime. She has earned the right to behave with far less restraint than she does, and yet she still remains composed."

Claire's head dropped, ashamed for not showing more compassion toward the Countess' situation. She felt Botley's tender hand lift her chin so she was looking into his pale grey eyes.

"And do not be so hard on yourself. You could not possibly know all that she has endured. That is why you are here."

Claire's rigid face broke into a smile. Not wanting to remain in the moment, she continued down the hall.

Finally, they approached the Countess' study door. Claire snickered, dreading confronting the woman who was holding her captive. She stared at the door for several seconds. Botley finally opened it.

"It really will be all right. Her bark is much worse than her bite. Besides, you are a very strong young woman who could handle much harder situations than listening to another person's stories."

"You think so?"

Botley closed his eyes and when they opened again, he had a proud look about him.

"I know so," he said.

"Thank you," Claire said then looked into the sun-filled study. Soaking in the confident words, she felt rejuvenated. Nodding her head self-assuredly, she entered into the room with no more hesitation.

Chapter 11
"The Evil Fairy Godmother"

The room immediately felt warmer and more welcoming than the previous times Claire had been in there. The curtains were drawn and light was pouring in through the window behind the Countess' desk.

The Countess was not present, leaving Claire to explore the room freely for the first time.

Weaving through the little sitting area that was comprised of two small couches and a chair, Claire made her way to the north wall bookshelf. Her excitement got the best of her and she could no longer hold back from running her finger along the spines, reading the titles.

"They were my husband's collection," said the Countess, stepping into the room and closing the door behind her. "Though, as you can see, they did not all belong to him."

The Countess stood flawlessly and pointed to the bookshelf beside Claire.

At first, Claire was confused by what she was supposed to be looking for. She knelt down, following the Countess' gesture and noted the titles of the books. '*Myths and*

Legends, The Song of Night, The Other Side, authored by: The Baron C. Dupree.'

"*The Other Side* was my last book," Claire said aloud.

"By far your best work," the Countess hummed in a knowing voice. "But I have enjoyed all the Baron's stories." She looked back at the books on the shelf.

Side by side were five novels that were authored by the Baron C. Dupree.

Without hesitation, Claire carefully picked up the first book and flipped through the pages. Clearly someone had read it several times because the pages were worn and the cover was tattered.

"I am glad to see you are such a follower of my work," Claire stated without even a glance at the Countess. "I will not deny that I was surprised that anyone knew my identity outside of Victor and myself. I thought I was practically untraceable."

"Practically. Let us just pretend that it was a fluke that I found out who you were. Having said that, the person who made me privy to the information would not tell me what the 'C.' stood for. Would you care to enlighten me?"

Claire closed the book in her hand and placed it back on the shelf where she found it. She turned to the Countess for the first time since she entered the room and instantly froze. A wooden staff that curled perfectly at the top into the Countess' hands stood handsomely before the refined woman.

"Are you all right?" the Countess asked sounding a little jarred by Claire's reaction. "You look like you have seen a ghost."

"I do apologize, but I would be remiss if I did not say that your walking stick is almost as famous as the Queen's tale."

"Hmm," hummed the Countess and moved behind her desk.

Claire's eyes followed her. "If you wish me to tell this story accurately, I need full access to what little of the Queen's things are still here and any other tidbits of information you wish to bestow upon me . . ."

Claire eyed the cane once more before the Countess tucked it under her desk as she sat down in her chair.

"If you expect to hear stories of beatings, then I am afraid you are going to be cruelly disappointed."

"I expect nothing Countess, that is why I am good at my work and-"

"And?"

"That is why you chose me."

The Countess' head reared up so she was looking down her nose at Claire.

"Tell me I am wrong." Claire stated.

She could feel the Countess' scrutinizing eye look her over.

"You are not wrong."

"Good, now tell me about the Fairy Godmother."

The Countess pulled Isabella's book from the top drawer and placed it onto her desk. "I noticed that everywhere Isabella went, this book was in her hand. I did know that it was the last book that Charles gave her before he died. No doubt it has sentimental value.

"What concerned me more than anything else was how she seemed to think the characters in this book were real."

"Well to a young child, that does not seem so far fetched," said Claire, taking her seat in front of the desk.

"Maybe not, but you have to understand, they were the only things she would talk to. If I were to approach her, she would either tell her invisible friend what to tell me or she would ignore me completely. It was quite insufferable."

"You still have not told me how the Fairy Godmother came to be-"

"I am getting there," the Countess snapped.

She continued. "One night, Isabella had fallen asleep by the fireplace, as she commonly did. I carefully removed the book from her care and took a closer look at these characters she held so dear."

"What did you find?"

"The Fairy Queen only showed herself to children in times of great need; children who needed to escape their current situations."

The Countess leaned closer to Claire. "Children that needed to escape the evil witch," she said, pointing to herself.

Claire could feel the tension in the room rising as the stern woman allowed her fingers to spread across the page. The Countess' eyes redirected to the book. Claire could tell she was examining every inch of the enchanted character.

"I could feel my blood boil where I stood. However, instead of getting upset, I thought it might be easier to connect with Isabella by playing a role in her very twisted game of make believe.

"That night, I rummaged through all my old dresses until I came across one that looked very similar to the one in this book. I also found the shoes from my wedding. I thought them unique enough that Isabella might think they were magical."

"I bet you were a sight to behold."

Gossip

"Perhaps, but the outfit alone was not enough. I also covered my hair up with one of Charles's blond wigs. It was rather amusing.

"Once my disguise was complete, I glided up the spiral stairs until I found myself at her door. I was afraid she would figure out who I was and that I would lose more ground with her.

"I took a deep breath and knocked on the door. As you well know, she locked her door every night. When she approached, I could see her eye peer through the key hole."

"She did not even wait a moment before throwing open the door and embracing me."

"How was that for you?" asked Claire.

"It was a surprise and enjoyable for the moment. Without giving her a chance to speak I said, 'Hello young one. I hear that you are quite distressed by your current situation.'

"She said to me, 'Oh Fairy Godmother, I was afraid you had not heard my cries for your help. Now I know you are here to help rid me of my evil stepmother.'

"Without thinking about it, my hands clenched her arms tightly until she yelped. I released her, remembering that I had to play this part and not let her callous insults get in my way. 'How can I help you my child?' I asked her simply. 'Take my stepmother far, far away from me,' she replied.

"I tried to force a smile onto my face but I think even she could tell my disapproval."

"So, how did you handle it?"

"I said, 'Young one, you needn't wish for your stepmother's removal. That would be very unkind. Instead, why not try warming up to her?'

"'She will not understand me, Fairy Godmother. She is a cruel witch that cannot see me. She can only see the image she wants me to be.'

"'Perhaps you should wash away some of this dirt so that she can see the beautiful girl under there. I am sure she is not so evil as you have made her out to be.'

"She looked at me strangely. Confusion consumed her while her eyes studied me carefully. I thought for sure she had figured out what was going on."

"Did she?"

"Surprisingly, no. She said, 'Fairy Godmother, I believe that you are wrong. My evil stepmother will never see me as anything but a servant under her boot. She killed my father and I am next.'"

Engrossed by the Countess' story, Claire found herself biting the tip of her quill. The scene continued to play out in her mind.

"I know you are wondering the same thing I was back then," the Countess said, catching Claire's far off look. "Isabella was a troubled child, as I have already said."

"I am just unsure of how she could be so off the mark about you. What did you do next?"

"I wanted to stop arguing with Isabella for good. So I said, 'Little one, you needn't bother with that evil stepmother of yours. I will give you something that will protect you. Do you remember your mother's ball gown?

"She eagerly nodded her head. 'I placed an enchantment on it so that anytime you wear it your stepmother will not recognize you.

"'You mean I will be invisible?' she asked. 'No,' I replied. 'More like you will transform into such a beautiful princess that even Prince Fabian's breath will be swept away.

"I handed over the gown to her. Though it was beautiful, I noticed her attention was not on the dress anymore, but instead on my feet.

"'Where did you get those lovely glass slippers?'

"'From a land far away,' I said to her. The memory of Charles giving them to me right before our wedding came flooding back into my mind. I could instantly feel my eyes burning. I did everything in my power not to cry, but unfortunately, Isabella picked up on my sadness.

"'Why are you sad, Fairy Godmother?' She embraced me again, tightly.

"'I wiped the single tear from my cheek and rested my head down on hers, and said, 'I am sad because I almost forgot that these slippers are yours as well. I would hate to think I was going to leave without bestowing them to you.

"She looked up at me in such wonderment and awe. A smile covered her entire face. I thought to myself, how beautiful this moment is. I slid my shoes from my feet and handed them over to her.

"As she gawked at them, I smiled and said, 'I must go now.'

"'No,' she pleaded, but I knew I could not stay any longer.

"'I must go. However, should the day come when you really need me again, I will return.' Isabella did not fight me any further on the matter. I tucked her into her bed, blew out the candle and whispered, 'Now sleep, little one.'

"I slid out the door before another word could be spoken."

"The glass slippers ... were yours?"

"Yes."

"And if Prince Fabian tried it on your foot-" Claire started.

"They would have fit me perfectly," the Countess finished.

"Amazing." Claire's eyes popped with bewilderment.

"The only amazing part is the unique size of our feet. That is all."

"Maybe so, but there is one concern I have."

"What?" the Countess asked without looking at her.

"Years later, the Queen still despises you."

"All I have ever done is try to help that girl."

"It seems now being Queen, she succeeded admirably on her own."

The Countess slammed her hands down on her desk. "I brought you here to tell my side of this tale."

"Tricked me to stay here is more like it."

"I know this whole ordeal has you puzzled. I promise that all will become clear soon enough. And regarding your father..."

Claire rose quickly and walked the length of the study. She found herself once more in front of the Baron Dupree's novels and slid one off the shelf.

"I am really not the one to tell you," the Countess said sincerely.

Flipping through the pages, Claire came across a picture of a little girl with open arms running to her father, who was already prepared to receive the embrace.

"I spent a great deal of my life wondering who he was, my father," Claire said, looking at the picture lovingly.

"My mother was so intent on making up this man, this very lovely man, that she could call my father. All the time, I could tell by the waiver in her voice that he was not real."

"Did you ever tell your mother that you did not believe her?" asked the Countess.

"No." Claire slammed the book closed and slid it back on the shelf. "Not until after she died did I even take up the notion of finding him."

Claire walked back over to the desk and sat down. "You asked me why I am here, Countess. You already know the answer. I want to find out who my father is. I want to know if he ever thought of me or wondered how I am doing all these years."

The Countess smiled honestly. "I am sorry you suffered, my dear."

"Me too." Claire brushed an oncoming tear away from her eye and said, "We have gotten a little off track. Is there anything else to know about the Fairy Godmother?"

The Countess thought hard, then, clearing her throat, she said, "There was only one good thing of which I could think."

"Which was?"

"Several years later, on the ever-so-famous night at the masked ball, I was the only person that was able to recognize Isabella. And it all came from one glimpse of her shoes."

Chapter 12
"Best of friends"

Victor was resting comfortably in a chair, reading a book when Claire exited the Countess' study in the early afternoon.

"Well? How did it go?" he asked her, cheerfully.

Claire moved across the hallway and looked out the window next to him, without saying a word.

"That good, huh?"

"She troubles me," Claire said simply.

Victor chuckled lightly and turned his attention back to his book. "Honestly, Claire, everyone you cannot figure out immediately troubles you. In fact, I would say you have spent your whole life being troubled."

Claire looked away from him, slightly annoyed with his honesty.

"Hmmmm hm hm hmmm. Mmm mmm m mmmmmmmm," was heard from outside, before Claire caught a glimpse of Josephine.

She was in her nightgown, twirling around in circles down in the garden below. Her long, untidy hair flew through the air as the girl continuously spun around and around.

"Dummm dumpty dumm. Mmmmm mmm," she hummed again.

"What is that bizarre noise?" Victor asked, still pretending to read his book.

Claire couldn't help but laugh at the odd girl's behavior. "It is only Josephine." Claire's eyes widened with intrigue. "Josephine," she muttered again under her breath, and then took off down the hall.

"Wait!" Victor called after her. "Who on earth is Josephine?"

* * *

Pushing through the courtyard doors, Claire stepped out into the secret garden. Victor was only a couple steps behind her.

Walking briskly down the pathway, she only half cared if Victor could keep up with her. Nonetheless, he tagged along.

"Is Josephine that odd creature still in her nightgown even though it is one o'clock?"

Claire placed a hand over his mouth though her attention was focused to the little patch of grass where Josephine was putting flowers in her hand.

Moving closer, Claire could see Josephine was taking the stem of each flower she picked and intertwining them together to make a small wreath for her head. As she strung the flowers together she sang a lively tune.

"When the sun shines, all the girls will look pretty. When the sun shines, all the girls will dance. When the sun shines, all the girls will be giddy. When the sun shines, she will take a chance."

Claire plucked a flower and held it out to her. Josephine took it and incorporated it into her wreath like she had picked it herself.

"Josephine?"

Josephine continued to sing and pick flowers, not paying Claire any attention. "When all the girls laugh, the world laughs too. When all the girls sing, the world listens in. When all the girls cry, the world is blue. When all the girls die, her world comes to an end."

"I am going to venture a guess and say she does not hear you," Victor chimed in.

Claire elbowed him in the side before moving next to Josephine and knelt beside her.

"I wish to speak with you about Isabella," she said, not sure if Josephine would comprehend.

Josephine's eyes flickered up momentarily but then looked back down at the almost-completed wreath in her hand.

"Nothing lost is nothing gained. Love is all that will remain. In loss and love is all to blame."

An uncomfortable silence settled in, though Josephine's hands continued to stay busy putting the final touches on her masterpiece.

"Well, I am glad we got that out of the way," Victor jabbed sarcastically.

"Shh," Claire hissed at him. He raised his hands in surrender.

"She was your friend, was she not?" Claire said, leaning closer.

Josephine held out the wreath and rested it comfortably on top of Claire's head.

"Thank you."

But before she could go any further, Josephine jumped to her feet and ran barefooted down the path and out of sight.

"Strange girl," Victor reiterated while Claire pulled the wreath off her head and took a closer look at it.

"I believe she knows more than anyone else in this house," Claire said, rising from the ground.

"She does indeed," came a soft, majestic voice.

When Claire and Victor turned, Genevieve was standing on the path, watching them.

"You must be Monsieur Krouse," Genevieve said, extending her hand out to Victor.

He gladly took and kissed it. "It is my pleasure, Fräulein."

Claire rolled her eyes at Victor's sad attempt to be charismatic.

"Fräulein Genevieve has asked for my help in finding a friend of hers," Claire mentioned.

"We would be happy to be of service," he hummed and flashed a flirtatious smile toward Genevieve.

Claire marveled at the beautiful headdress in her hand. The red and white flowers were perfectly sized between large and small, making an intricate pattern.

"Despite Josephine's oddities, she is quite an artist," Genevieve interjected. "She is the one who painted that picture in my mother's study."

"The only painting I saw in there was a family portrait."

Genevieve looked at her, baffled. "It is the other painting by the window."

"The Countess did hide something from me the first night I was here. Perhaps that is it."

"That would not surprise me. Mother always has an order to the way she does things."

"Does that order always involve keeping people captive at your house?" Claire asked, a little agitated.

Genevieve attempted to smile but it looked painful. "Come, let us walk a bit. I will tell you what I can about Isabella."

"I would like that," Claire approved, while Victor trailed behind the two women.

"Isabella spent most of her time alone when we first met her. I could tell she had a playful spirit but she would not share any of it with Josephine or myself. Having said that, after a short period of time she saw the obscurity of Josephine and took to her. The two started playing together."

"Did you feel left out?" Claire asked.

"At first, no. I was just happy for Josephine to be making a friend. She, too, spends a lot of time alone because she has not been well the whole of her life."

"Is she . . . ?" Claire hesitated.

"She is different. That is the only way I can ever think of my sister."

"Does she ever say anything that makes sense?"

"Everything she says makes sense. You just have to think harder about her words than you would in a regular conversation. I know a lot of people disagree with me, but what she says does have meaning."

"It sounds like you have understood her before," Claire interjected.

"Well, I remember when my father had just passed. I cried so hard that my whole body ached. I could not be around anyone for days. One night Josephine snuck into my room while I was asleep and laid her head on my chest. I was startled awake.

"'What are you doing here, Jo?' I asked her. She sang something to me that to this day I will never forget."

The group stopped on the path, now seeing Josephine playing in another patch of grass in the garden. Genevieve broke off and went and sat next to her younger sister.

Clearing her throat, Genevieve sang, "Father has gone on a trip so far. Father has gone—no one to blame. Father has gone on his own mar. But Father still loves you all the same."

Genevieve kept staring at her sister. Josephine looked like she had lost control of her arms as she let them fly in every direction.

One last kiss on her sister's forehead, and Genevieve returned to the group. Claire noticed the color in Genevieve's cheeks were gone.

"Even after all the time that has passed since that night, I still get choked up when I think about it."

"There is nothing wrong with knowing your father loves you," said Claire.

"What was your father like? I imagine an adventurous and good man by the looks of you."

Claire chuckled lightly. "I wish I could tell you, but I did not know him. My mother raised me. From what little she told me before she died, she was from Paris but got into some sort of trouble."

"Trouble?" Genevieve repeated.

"Again, my mother was not very forthcoming. After she was pregnant with me, she snuck over the border into Germany and settled in the town of Stuttgart. That is how I know Victor. His family owns a large vineyard there and they allowed my mother and me to occupy a small cottage on the edge of their land."

"Did you ever find your father?"

Claire's whole body stiffened.

"Why are you asking me this?" Claire inquired. "Do you know my father?"

"No, Mademoiselle Du Bois. It is just ... having missed my own father all my life, I feel for those who are in a similar situation. I will not ask you any more questions," Genevieve said and bowed her head apologetically.

At the last word, thoughts flew through Claire's mind. Her eyes roamed uncontrollably around the courtyard, bouncing between Josephine in the grass and Genevieve's perfect form standing next to her. Finally, her eyes came to rest on the empty window in front of the Countess' study.

"Genevieve, do you know how to get us out of the house without the Countess knowing?"

Genevieve nodded her head.

"I smell trouble," Victor insinuated.

"I think it is time we go to town."

Genevieve's face soured. "You do know that the Queen will find you as soon as you step off the grounds?"

"She cannot possibly have a guard watching the house all the time," Claire argued.

"You might be surprised," Victor said, gesturing to the cut on his head.

Claire took his hands into hers, "Come on, Victor. What I need to know cannot be learned in this house. I must go to town. Please!"

"This is lunacy," Victor started, "But I will do it. I will take that risk for my dear friend."

"I hate when you talk to me like that," said Claire.

Victor defiantly crossed his arms. Claire hugged him despite his opposition.

"Is this what love looks like these days? It has been so long since I have seen it," Genevieve chuckled.

Claire and Victor both jumped and said, "Oh no, no, no. We are not together."

"Uh huh," hummed Genevieve with a quizzical brow and looked at both of them as if they were lying.

"Tonight, will you come and get me through the secret passage?" Claire asked, trying to change the subject.

"Once the house has settled, I will help you out to the edge of the estate. Now, if you will excuse me."

Genevieve bowed to the two and made her way down the path leaving Victor and Claire a moment to themselves.

As soon as she was out of sight, Claire's smile quickly faded. "Why can we not just be friends?" Claire growled.

"I could think of far worse people you could be courting than me," Victor pointed out.

Claire rolled her eyes until Josephine regained her attention. The strange girl was now standing up and spinning in circles. The once soft tune she was singing grew louder and louder.

"Trouble is brewing, Love is stewing. And we are all going to tumble down, down, down."

With the last words, Josephine fell hard to the ground and laid still.

Victor shook his head, "Strange girl."

Chapter 13
"Late Night Stroll"

Three cloaked figures made their way across the front lawn of the Countess De Leon's estate under the shroud of night. As they approached the stone wall, Genevieve slowed her pace.

"This is where I must leave you," she said softly.

Genevieve pulled back a curtain of ivy, exposing the eroded wall space that Claire and Victor could easily climb through.

"Thank you," Claire whispered.

Genevieve bowed her head and said, "Make sure you stay off the main roads or Isabella will certainly find you. Now go. Quickly."

Claire looked one last time on the Countess' house before she and Victor squeezed through the wall.

* * *

The trees along the road were quite dense, barely allowing the moonlight to shine through. Even though Claire wished to heed Genevieve's suggestion about not taking the main road, she knew that it was the only hope she had of getting to the heart of town.

Claire allowed her hands to dangle at her sides, just clipping the top of the long, wild grass that grew alongside the road.

"So, what is your plan?" Victor asked. "I am sure you have one by now."

"We are going to speak with some of the town's people, to see how they viewed the Countess before Isabella became Queen."

"That sounds like a brilliant idea," Victor scoffed. "Why do we not just go into the most populated pub, hold out our hands and say, 'Please arrest me, how I do so love the stocks.'"

"I do not know how I have put up with you for twenty years."

Victor drew so close to her that for a moment, Claire thought that he was going to kiss her. His nose nuzzled her ears and she could feel the warmth of his breath as he said, "I guess I am just that charming."

A ball of laughter exploded from his lips and he elbowed her hard in the arm.

"Hmm," Claire grunted. "I hate you, Victor Krouse."

"I know," he grinned.

A rustle went through the grass. Claire turned with ears perked.

Victor put a caring hand around her shoulders.

"It is just the wind, my dear friend."

All of a sudden, a figure jumped out of the brush behind Victor and put a knife to his throat.

"Then again, I may have underestimated the violent brush of France," he said, trying to make light of the dangerous situation he was now in.

"Empty your pockets," demanded an older woman's voice.

"We are not carrying anything of value," Claire said, hastily.

The knife at Victor's throat pulled tighter to his skin.

"Wait!" Claire shouted. She pulled a necklace off her neck and held it out. "Take this."

The woman peeked over Victor's shoulder at the trinket held out to her. Letting go and shoving Victor to the ground, the woman swooped the necklace out of Claire's hand.

She quickly put it between her teeth and bit on it. "Real gold," she muttered. Then laying it flat in her hand, she held it up to one of the little beams of moonlight that made its way through the leaves.

Her eyes widened at the emblem engraved on the little charm around the chain. The woman held her dagger up to Claire, pointing it right at her face.

"Are you Isabella?" she demanded.

"What?" Claire said, a little taken aback.

"Are you Queen Isabella?" the woman hissed.

"Do not be ridiculous. My name is Claire Du Bois."

The woman lunged at Claire but Victor jumped in the way and knocked the woman to the ground.

"What is your problem?" Victor said, as the woman swung her knife at him and he ducked out of the way.

She lunged again. This time, Victor caught her arm and twisted it behind her back until the knife fell out of her hand.

"Tell me what this is about," Victor said in a more serious tone. "Why are you attacking us?"

"She is Queen Isabella," the woman said, gesturing with her head to Claire. "She has oppressed my people."

"Oppressed what people?" Claire asked.

"The gypsies."

Victor's grip loosened until the woman could wiggle free.

"I am not the Queen," reiterated Claire. "But I am most interested to know why you think so."

The gypsy woman held up the necklace.

"It is just a symbol, it does not mean anything," said Claire.

"Just a symbol?" The woman looked at her in disbelief. "Just a—? This is the symbol of Le roi Childebert; only the king and queen would be permitted this kind of a trinket."

Claire and Victor looked at each other in confusion, then back to the woman for further explanation.

"Le roi Childebert had only a handful of these emblem necklaces made and gave them to his children. They have grown to be seen as the mark of royalty."

"You are mad, woman," Claire said, a little unsure.

"I very well might be, but whoever gave you this stole it from the royal family."

Claire broke the silence with a hearty chuckle. "Preposterous. My mother was no thief and certainly would have never stolen from the King and Queen."

"Mmm," the gypsy murmured, looking back down at the necklace. "As much as I would like to take this from you, I think I will be safer if you keep it."

The woman dropped the necklace into Claire's hand and closed it. Claire didn't even hesitate in putting it back around her neck, keeping her focus on the gypsy woman.

"I take it you have never met the Queen, if you mistook me for her?"

"I have not. Only..."

"Yes?"

"As I understand, the Queen is a very clean woman. Constantly cleaning her body."

"Yes?"

"There is only one other creature I could describe like that. There was a little girl many years ago. I used to go down by the river with my crafts and make simple jewelry. She came down to the river to wash her dress.

"She did not pay me any mind, nor did I care. She was more interested in getting that tattered dress clean."

"Who cares about such nonsense?" Victor interjected.

"I guess no one of consequence," retorted the gypsy woman. "I just thought it odd that she cleaned the same dress for four hours."

Claire looked over at Victor, "That certainly sounds like the Queen."

"It was before she was Queen, to be sure. I hear she wears nicer frocks now," pointed out the woman.

The woman spun around to look down the empty road. Claire and Victor followed suit. All was still until Claire heard footsteps running away from her. By the time she had turned, the gypsy woman had already disappeared into the brush.

"Do not show that necklace to anyone. It will be your neck if you do," And with that, the gypsy woman was gone.

Claire lifted the necklace to her eyes to examine the emblem.

The sound of *clip clop* came from a short distance away.

Both Claire and Victor quickly pulled their cloaks over their heads and stood off to the side of the road. No more than a minute passed before a troop of ten royal guards on horseback came marching up to them.

"You there," one of them shouted. "What are you doing traveling so late?"

Victor cleared his throat and, in the worst French accent Claire had ever heard, he said, "Is it a crime to have an evening stroll with my lady friend?"

Claire lifted her hand to her lips, trying desperately to suppress the oncoming laughter.

"Your lady friend?" the guard repeated.

"Oui, Monsieur," Victor said, and then pulled Claire close to him.

Claire chortled nervously.

"She seems in good spirits. Perhaps your lady friend would care to entertain us," stated the guard, and looked at his fellow guards behind him with a smirk. They all started laughing. The guard leaned forward to Claire. "What do you say? Do you care to join us?"

Victor tucked Claire behind him, and said, "Why would she want to accompany a horse's ass, Monsieur?" Claire pulled on his arm, disapproving of the jabbing comment.

The guard stopped laughing and looked at him, insulted.

"What are you doing?" Claire whispered to Victor. "You are going to get us arrested."

"What did you say?" the guard growled, jumping from his horse.

Victor pulled his arm away from Claire and walked closer to the guard.

"I can already tell from your poor accent that you are either uneducated or foreign," started the guard. "or maybe both."

Victor's cloaked head bobbed up and down as he nodded. "At least I have enough intelligence to know when I am talking to the village idiot," Victor said in his native tongue.

The guard grabbed Victor's cloak and yanked it back from his head. "You!"

"Me!" Victor threw the first blow, hitting the guard right in the face. The other guards hopped off their horses and grabbed Victor by the arms. The head guard rose from the ground.

Standing in front of Victor, he punched him right in the stomach, knocking the wind out of him. Victor doubled over, gasping for air. The head guard grabbed Victor by the hair and yanked his head backward.

"You never learn. Perhaps I should give you a better lesson this time."

"You think you can teach me?" Victor laughed. "Before, I was just mocking, but you really are the village idiot."

The head guard punched Victor in the face not once but twice. When he reached back to punch him one more time, a rope wrapped around the head guard's wrist and yanked him backward.

"This is no way to treat guests of the King and Queen, now is it?" said a stern male voice, just before kicking his horse's sides. He took off, dragging the head guard behind him.

The two guards holding onto Victor promptly let him go.

"That is what I thought," said Victor through his blood-covered lips.

Claire ran to his side. "Last night I was so worried about you and now..."

Victor looked at her with a half smile.

"You are such a fool!"

When Claire rose, she looked down the road at the man on the horse riding back toward them.

He brought his horse to a halt next to the rest of the guards. "Pick him up on your way back," he barked, giving them a stern look. The group of royal guards quickly jumped on their horses and rode away.

The man dismounted his horse. Turning his attention to Claire and Victor, he spoke. "Gute nacht, Fräulein Du Bois."

"Good evening, indeed,' Claire responded in her native tongue, impressed. 'You speak German?"

The man nodded. "But it is probably safer if we speak in French."

"Oui," Claire agreed.

He removed his hat and swooped into a bow. "I am the Captain of the royal guard."

Claire curtsied. "And you know my name?"

"I believe everyone in town knows your name. You and Monsieur Krouse are quite famous already. I must admit," he continued, "You are far prettier than the rumors had let on."

Claire blushed at his words.

The Captain took Claire's hand into his and kissed it. Victor cleared his throat loudly while breaking between them.

"Ah, yes. Monsieur Krouse.' The Captain spoke. 'This is—what—the second time I have saved you recently?"

Victor took Claire by the arm.

"Ah," the Captain said. "I am sorry, I did not know you were together."

"We are not together," Claire argued. But when she tried to pull away from Victor, she felt his tight grip holding her close.

Victor's cool eyes darted over to Claire. The Captain looked back and forth between them. "Either way, I am afraid I must escort you to the castle. The Queen is most anxious to meet you."

Claire could feel her heart racing again but she wasn't sure if it was from worry or from the excitement of meeting the odd girl that had been the center of almost every discussion.

The Captain grabbed the reins of the head guard's horse. "Here; I am sure Monsieur Monte would be more than honored for you to ride his horse."

"I have it from here," Victor said to the Captain and then held his hand out to Claire.

"Men," she breathed.

After Claire had mounted the horse, Victor climbed on behind her.

"I hope you are ready," he whispered in her ear. "You are about to get what you wanted."

Claire smiled. "I know."

With a smack of the reins, the trio trotted toward the castle.

Chapter 14
"Clean Hands"

The trio approached the entrance gate to the castle. Two guards stood to either side, barely flinching. Claire caught their glares as she rode past them.

"Hmmm, word does travel fast," she whispered over her shoulder to Victor.

The group came to a full stop in front of the grand staircase leading to the front door of the castle. The ten royal guards that they encountered earlier that evening were standing at attention in two rows off to the side.

"Here we are," the Captain said, dismounting his horse.

Victor jumped off the back of their horse and helped Claire down. As they walked past the royal guards, Claire noticed the head guard standing at the end had fresh bruises and scrapes on his face. She wasn't sure if Victor got a clean hit on him or if it was from the Captain dragging him off down the road.

"Mademoiselle Du Bois, Monsieur Krouse, this is one of my finest swordsmen, Francis Monte," said the Captain, gesturing to the beaten-up guard.

The man did not flinch but he did glower at them. The Captain patted the guard on the shoulder and looked back at Claire.

"He is a good man, though still a little ill-tempered at times," the Captain said with a snicker. "Shall we?"

The Captain led the way up the stairs and into the entrance hall of the castle. More royal guards met the group, two of whom seized Victor by the arms.

"No!" Claire screamed and pathetically attempted to pull a rather large guard off of Victor. "What are you doing?"

The Captain took Claire by the hand and pulled her away. "Mademoiselle, it is you the Queen wants to meet. Not him."

"Where will he be taken?" Claire asked with concern.

"Somewhere safe. I promise."

The Captain nodded his head and the guards started to escort Victor down the hall.

"Victor!" Claire screamed after him.

Victor looked over his shoulder and winked at her, then faced forward again. "Stop worrying, Claire. I have it under control."

Claire looked back at the Captain and said, "Of course he does."

The Captain held out his arm to her. With great apprehension, Claire took it.

The two entered into the throne room. Looking around, no more than a handful of servants tending to cleaning and polishing the statues were present. At the far end sat a tiny figure of a woman sitting perfectly on her throne.

The Captain led her across the length of the room. Her eyes surveyed the magnificence of the hall. Large tapestries with the King's many accomplishments hung from every wall, and on the floor was an intricately-designed Persian rug. Gold-plated torches adorned every column next to the statues, and a few guards were stationed throughout the room.

As they walked, she couldn't help but notice that all the servants stopped and whispered to each other and some even pointed at her.

"Leave us!" the Queen said. The servants' eyes dropped to the floor and they resigned from the room

Finally, the two reached the bottom of the small set of stairs that led to the elegantly-decorated thrones. Claire caught the pumpkin etched in the back of the King's empty chair. Then her eyes flitted over to Queen Isabella.

Getting a closer look, Claire observed the beautiful young woman's long, blond hair with a diamond-studded crown resting comfortably on top. Her face appeared to be soft and gentle but her eyes were tormented and dangerous.

Claire bowed her head as the Captain stepped off to the side of the hall.

"How do you find yourself this evening, Mademoiselle Du Bois?" the Queen asked.

"I am quite well, thank you. And you, Your Majesty?"

The Queen shifted slightly in her seat looking down at her clasped hands.

"I wish I could say I was well, but there is something gnawing at me this evening."

The Queen rose, and moved delicately but deliberately toward Claire as she spoke.

"It seems that my stepmother has been telling lies about me again. I thought she had stopped that horrible habit years ago, but here you are."

"I do not understand," Claire said simply, keeping eye contact with her.

The Queen came to stand right next to her. Looking out at the room that lay beyond, she whispered into Claire's ear, "We both know why you are here. Even if you do not admit it to me, I am sure your friend will."

Claire turned and looked at the malice in the Queen's eyes.

"I came to find out the truth," said Claire.

"Yes, well, the truth is in the eye of the beholder, is it not?"

Claire stood strong. "If you can recall, Your Majesty, I was not raised in this land. I do not care for French folklore or fairy tales."

"Everyone likes a good fairy tale."

"If I am not mistaken, I believe more accurately that you like a good fairy tale."

"Watch yourself, Mademoiselle Du Bois."

The Queen, for the first time since she entered the room, looked Claire in the eyes. "I am capable of many things."

"I have no doubt of your power, Your Majesty. Please know that I am here to get facts; not stories. If there is something you wish to tell me, by all means, I am listening."

The Queen raised her fingers to her lips, a little taken aback. "Really?" she murmured.

"Really."

The Queen gestured with her hand to a squire who was standing against a column on the side of the room. He quickly grabbed a golden bowl of piping hot water, a bar of soap, and a towel, which he draped over his arm.

Without dropping a single bit of water, he brought it over.

The Queen carefully placed her hands in it, took the bar of soap, and scrubbed them clean. It took several minutes for her to clean every individual finger and then she wiped them dry. After she had completed this ceremony, she turned her focus back to Claire, who was still standing in front of her.

"I have no doubt that you know the fairy tale that followed shortly after I was made Queen."

"Of course."

"I will admit that it was an enchanting fairy tale indeed, but, like so many tales, a lot of details were left out."

"What kinds of details?" Claire asked, genuinely interested.

"She hit me."

"Excuse me?" Claire said in disbelief.

"She hit me!" the Queen said loud enough that it echoed through the room.

Not convinced and unaware, Claire's brow rose as she studied the Queen.

"You do not believe me?"

"Everyone has a tale to tell," Claire pointed out. Then, reaching in her satchel, she dug around for some parchment. When she finally pulled some out, the emerald ring Josephine gave her fell out too.

The Queen knelt down and snatched it into her hand. All of a sudden her mouth fell agape and her face contorted with anger. "How did you get this?"

Lost for a good explanation, Claire said the first thing that came to mind. "The Countess gave it to me as a gift."

"Liar!" the Queen growled. Her eyes became narrow and her head tilted in such a way that she looked like she was going to attack Claire.

Claire tried not to falter. "She did. However, if it has some significance to you, please take it."

The Queen threw the ring back at Claire and luckily, she caught it. Quickly, she shoved it back in her bag.

"Keep that piece of filth out of my sight," the Queen said snidely. "And I do not wish to talk to someone who has been seduced by that evil witch."

"You wanted me here, Your Mejesty, or you would not have tormented my friend nor had your guard come looking for us. The Countess, despite her flaws—"

"The Countess means nothing to me! Captain, come take Mademoiselle Du Bois to her room!"

"What?"

"I need time to think before I speak further with you."

"You must be joking," Claire chuckled.

The Queen's whole body became rigid and her upper lip curled back into a sneer.

"Maybe tomorrow I will be in a better mood to 'tell you my tale.' Captain!"

Without any hesitation, the Captain immediately moved to Claire's side.

"Yes, Your Mejesty?"

"Take Mademoiselle Du Bois to her room and make sure she stays there until morning."

He bowed. "Yes, Your Mejesty."

The Captain held out his hand and gestured for Claire to move toward the door. As they were walking, Claire could hear the Queen talking to herself.

"Who was that, my dear?" came a low male voice.

Gossip

When she glanced over her shoulder, she saw a young man who was a little older than the Queen, stepping out from a side door. When her eyes first fell upon the King, her stomach bottomed out and she thought she was going to be sick, for the striking resemblance between the King and herself was unmistakable.

Dizziness consumed her and her thoughts became unfocused. "It cannot be," she muttered.

"What was that?" the Captain asked. But there was no response.

When he turned to her, Claire was ghost white and her steps were unsteady.

"Mademoiselle?"

Claire didn't even look at him, caught in a trance. "The Countess knew all along . . . my father was the king."

The last thing she felt was her legs giving way underneath her.

Chapter 15
"The King's Mistress"

The Captain opened up a double door and led Claire out onto the terrace.

"I think some fresh air will do you good," the Captain said to her.

She slowly breathed in the cool night air, bringing some calm back to her nerves.

"Sit here," the Captain suggested. "Take a moment to collect yourself."

"Thank you," Claire said, still trying to take everything in.

A symphony of crickets chirped in the air and the moonlight still shone brightly, enough that no candles were needed to see the Captain as they talked.

"Feeling better?" he finally said.

"Much," Claire said, not truly believing her own words.

"If I may ask, what happened just now?"

Claire's eyes rushed up to meet the Captain's. "I saw the King."

Gossip

The Captain paused before letting out a long sigh. "Judging by your reaction you did not know, and I see no point in keeping this from you."

"Please tell me," Claire said, almost pleading.

"As you can tell, I am far too young to have been there when you were born. Having said that, your mother is well known amongst all the servants for her kindness."

"That is why all those servants were looking at me when we entered the throne room."

The Captain bowed his head. "Very observant of you. Yes, you look just like her, you know? Your mother."

Claire looked down, made uncomfortable by the compliment.

"You see, the other mistresses of the King took his gifts and enjoyed him spoiling them. Most tended to treat everyone poorly, especially the servants. Your mother, on the other hand, was a kind woman who gave all but one gift to them. She understood the harshness of a servant's life."

Claire bit her lower lip. "Was this the one gift she kept?" She held up the medallion hanging on the chain around her neck.

Again, the Captain bowed his head in confirmation.

"Why would the King send her away?"

"He did not send her away. She left on her own accord. There was no doubt in anyone's mind that the King loved your mother more than any of his other women, even Queen Sophia."

"Then, what happened?"

The Captain shrugged. "From what I understand, after she learned that the Queen was pregnant, she vanished."

"Vanished?" Claire repeated.

"She snuck from her chambers and out of the castle. Everyone claimed they did not know where she had gone. Though, it is common knowledge amongst the servants that she had help from not only her handmaidens but also some of the cooks and groundskeepers. It was the least they could do for all her kindness. After she was gone, they were sworn to secrecy."

"It does not make sense," Claire chimed in. "Why would she leave if the King loved her so much?"

"As rumor has it, he never knew of her pregnancy." The Captain sat down next to Claire on the cement bench. He handed her a handkerchief for the oncoming tears.

"He never knew you were born. What I can tell you is that life after your mother's disappearance was dreadful for everyone. The King's anger was taken out on his people. He only found joy again after Prince Fabian was born."

Claire sniffled into the handkerchief. Tears fell freely down her cheeks.

"You were kind to tell me all this," Claire sobbed.

The Captain put his arms around her. "You are an important part of this country's history, Claire. The least you can do is know it."

Claire rose from her seat and began to drift across the balcony as she spoke. "You seem to be in the know."

"When I was younger, I traveled all over Asia and eastern Europe."

"That is why you can speak German." Claire interjected.

The Captain smiled at her and then continued. "I studied a lot—I learned language, certainly, philosophy, fighting techniques, and the value of paying attention."

"How did you end up here in Paris?"

"This is my home. I was born just outside the city walls."

"And when you came back you joined the royal guard?"

The Captain looked at Claire with an amused smile. "You could say, it kind of fell into my lap."

After wandering halfway across the balcony during the conversation, Claire made her way back to the bench on which the Captain was still resting and sat down next to him.

"Do you mind telling me the story?"

The Captain leaned back against the wall behind him in thought. The moonlight still captured his strong, determined chin perfectly.

"The first thing I heard after crossing the French border was that Prince Fabian was having a masked ball for all eligible ladies in the kingdom. Everyone in the town was going to be there, and I thought it might be a great way to—" he stopped, seeming to be looking for the right words.

"—reacquaint myself with Paris. When I came upon the gate, it was late in the evening. I tried to get into the ball, but the guard was relentless about only letting in guests with invitations. I thought about climbing over the wall but there were guards posted too close together to make a safe entry.

"I had only been trying to get in for about five minutes or so before the midnight bells rang. I figured the festivities would be winding down shortly and there was no point in staying much longer.

"Just as the thought ran through my mind, the now Queen Isabella came running from the gates frantically. She lost her footing and fell flat on her face. During that fall, her shoe went flying from her foot and landed on the ground.

"She hurried into her carriage and rode off down a hidden path as quickly as possible. As Prince Fabian came running out, he scooped up her tiny glass slipper into his hand and screamed, 'Find her, find that girl! There will be a reward for the man who can bring me that girl!'

"I was the only one who saw which way she had gone. I pushed my horse to catch her carriage and I did with no trouble. Still, I stayed out of sight. Finally, the carriage pulled off the road and into the back gate of the Countess De Leon's estate.

"I tied off my horse and snuck over the wall. I saw her slip into the house while, the butler it looked like, pulled the carriage into the barn. That was the last I saw her that night."

Claire leaned forward, enthralled with the Captain's memory of the ever-famous night. "Please continue," she breathed with excitement.

"The next morning, I learned quickly about how desperate the Prince was to find the identity of his mysterious guest. I knew immediately what had to be done.

"Now being daytime, it was easier to see the weaknesses in the walls around the castle and there were no guards stationed at the top like there had been the previous night. I simply found the lowest point and climbed over. Once I was in, I just needed to find the Prince and hope he would hear me out.

"I did not make it but a couple of steps before one of the guards saw me. They chased me all the way through the front doors and into the entrance hall of the castle. I had reached my hand up for the throne room door when two guards tackled me down to the ground. I struggled to break free but they were much larger than I."

"You must have done something valiant. You are now the Captain of the royal guard."

"Of course. I found the King his bride. While lying on the floor under the mass of two large guards, I screamed so loud that I think the whole castle could hear me. The Prince came stomping out of a side room with a small group of his advisors."

"So, he was not even in the throne room?"

"I was just as surprised, but no, he was not. He looked down at me struggling and said, 'What is the meaning of this intrusion?' The guard said, 'Nothing, Sire. Just some beggar wanting some food.'

"'Not true,' I shouted right before I was punched in the face by the same guard. 'Get him out of here,' the Prince spouted. But then I screamed again, 'I know her! I know the girl you seek.'

"The Prince quickly spun on his heel and studied me closely. He did not move for several moments, but then came over and knelt down beside me. 'You know her?' he whispered. I nodded my head the best I could.

"'Here is the deal I will strike with you. If you can show me where she is, I will raise your station to my royal guard. After all, you were clever enough to get all the way into the entrance hall unscathed.'

"I could feel the weight of the guards on top of me baring down at the comment. Clearly, they were not as pleased with how clever I was.

"'What say you?' Prince Fabian asked with more kindness than I would expect he shares with most peasants. I nodded in agreement.

"'Very well, let him up,' he ordered.

"'The girl that you seek is at the Countess De Leon's estate.' The next thing I knew, two of the Prince's advisors scurried out the front door. 'You will wait here with me,' he said calmly. I knew then he was sizing me up and hoping that I was right in knowing where to find his future queen."

"And you were right," Claire acknowledged.

"Less than an hour later Isabella was brought to the castle where she told her sad life story to the Prince, and shortly after, the two were married."

"That is quite an impressive story," Claire said, still caught up in it all.

"One for the ages, to be sure. And I can think of no better place to tell you all this," he admitted.

Claire looked at him, puzzled.

The Captain clasped his hands together before moving to the center of the large balcony and spinning around. "Look around you."

She turned in every direction taking in the beautiful marble terrace until at last her eyes landed on the clock tower right next to them. She rose, excitedly. "This is where they danced."

The Captain nodded.

Claire moved toward the Captain. "Do you dance, Captain?"

The Captain's eyes dropped to the ground.

"Victor does not care for it much either," she noted.

"You two are an interesting couple," the Captain admitted.

Claire let out a little huff. "Why does everyone say that? We are not together."

The Captain crossed his arms, standing very firmly in place. "Have you not noticed how much he protects you?"

"No more than he would protect his sister," Claire said dismissively.

The Captain walked over to Claire and offered his arm to her.

"Would you care to put a wager on that?" the Captain offered. "I would be more than happy to prove it to you."

Claire looked away, agitated. "I do not think that is necessary."

"That is because you already know it to be true."

Finally taking his arm, she sighed. "I did not come to France so strangers could tell me how to act around my dear friend."

The Captain chuckled.

"Fine!" Claire snapped. "Put it to a test, but you are wasting your time."

The two started across the balcony toward the entrance to the castle.

"I do not believe so, Mademoiselle Du Bois. You will see. There will come a time when Victor will put his life in danger to save yours."

"He is foolish is all."

The Captain continued forward, "What kind of men are we, if not fools in love?"

Chapter 16
"The Queen's Tale"

A loud rap at the bedchamber door startled Claire awake.

Upon opening it, Claire saw the Captain standing alone in the hall. He bowed.

"Mademoiselle, I am sorry for waking you, but the King and Queen would like to see you now."

Claire yawned and wiped the sleep from her eyes.

"Of course. I will get dressed immediately."

Just as she said this, two young lady's maids snuck past her into the room carrying an elegant dress and shoes.

"We will return with Victor shortly."

Not showing much propriety in her curtsey, Claire yawned again before shutting the door.

Half an hour passed before the anticipated knock came. Sure enough, the Captain and his guards stood just as they had before, except, Victor now stood behind him.

"Victor!" Claire said in an excited tone and leapt into the hall, hugging her friend.

"Unf," Victor grunted on the impact.

"Sorry," Claire said, pulling away self-consciously.

"I do not mind the hug, just not so enthusiastically next time," Victor said with a grin.

Claire's eyes slid over to the Captain, who, unsurprisingly, had a raised brow.

"This way," he said, and started down the hall.

* * *

When they entered, Claire caught the attention of the many nobles congregated in the throne room. This time Claire was prepared for all eyes following her every move until they came before the King and Queen.

"Your Majesties," Claire said, and curtsied.

Before even a word was spoken, Claire could swear the King gasped when he saw her. She glanced up at him nervously.

"So, you are the one Isabella was telling me so much about last night," said the King. "She tells me that you have come a long way to be here today."

"Stuttgart," Claire murmured, sheepishly.

"Excuse me?"

"We are from Stuttgart, Your Mejesty," Victor said, stepping in.

Claire didn't even look at Victor but hoped that he wouldn't say anything that would get them into more trouble.

"Germany," King Fabian said quickly. "I do wonder what has brought you so far from home?"

"I am sure the Queen has told you that I am a guest of the Countess De Leon," said Claire timidly.

The whole room gasped and muttering flew from lip to lip. Claire looked around the room at all the shocked and concerned expressions.

King Fabian slammed a staff hard against the floor and it echoed throughout the hall. "Silence!" he screamed at his court.

The room obeyed, though an occasional heads still shook with disbelief.

"The Countess De Leon," the King retorted. "No one has talked to her in years. She has been caged up in that home of hers for quite some time. Who even knows if she still has all her faculties about her?"

The Court laughed at the King's joke. He looked around, pleased with himself.

"With all due respect, Your Highness, the Countess De Leon wanted to speak with me because I am a close friend with one of her favorite authors, the Baron Dupree."

"Nonsense," the Queen interjected. "She brought you here to tell lies."

Claire bowed her head, not wanting to make eye contact with either the King or Queen.

"My dear, please calm yourself," the King said, raising his hand to the Queen.

The Queen fell back in her chair with arms crossed, grimacing.

The King turned his attention once again to Claire. "The Baron Dupree, I am not familiar with him. Please, tell me why he interested the Countess so?"

Claire began biting her lower lip. "Well, you see, Your Majesty, the Baron is an author . . ."

"An author. Interesting, go on."

"Well the Countess wanted to . . . to . . ."

"It is all right. Go on," said the King, kindly encouraging her.

"She wanted to tell you lies, is that it?" snapped the Queen.

Gossip

"She wanted to . . ."

"Just say it! She wanted to tell you what a horrible little girl I was!"

"Well . . ." Claire stumbled over her words. Beads of sweat lined her forehead and her breathing grew heavy.

"What she means to say is that the Baron sent her here on his behalf. He wanted to know more about the ever-so-famous tale of the Queen and her evil stepmother," Victor said, stepping forward and taking Claire's hand into his.

Claire's eyes instantly dropped to their hands intertwined and then back up to look Victor in the face. He was not looking at her, but instead at the Queen.

"Why can she not answer for herself?" the Queen said sharply.

Victor smiled handsomely and bowed as he spoke. "Mademoiselle Du Bois is overwhelmed by your magnificence, Your Majesty. The story of the cruelty you suffered has reached even our ears in Germany."

The King grabbed the Queen's hand and kissed it, "See, you are famous all over Europe."

Claire looked over at Victor like a whipped puppy dog and mouthed the words 'thank you'. He squeezed her hand as if to say 'I have it under control.'

Victor stepped closer to the Queen with great interest and held out his hand to her. "Your Mejesty, we would be honored if you told us the story about the night you met the King."

Bewildered, the Queen took Victor's hand and rose. She walked down the few steps to the main floor and made her way to the middle of the room.

"When I was very young, my Fairy Godmother left me a dress and her magical glass slippers."

"Magical, you say?" Victor followed her to the middle of the room with enthusiasm.

The Queen leaned into him and with the most animated face, repeated, "Magical."

"That must have been something," Victor admitted.

"It was," agreed the Queen. "Many years later, the King was to have a masked ball. My evil stepmother promised me that I could go if I could finish all my chores."

"But that did not happen, did it?"

"No, it did not. I was all ready to go with them. When I came into the entrance hall, she struck me in the head. My body hit the staircase hard. Even now, I can remember the warmth of the blood dripping down the side of my face."

The Queen stepped closer to Victor, letting down her hair. It fell perfectly by her face. She pulled some strands on the right side of her head back and exposed a scar.

"Your Mejesty," Victor gasped. "I had no idea the Countess was capable of such cruelty."

The Queen's eyes wandered aimlessly while lost in the memory. "What little I can remember in my half-conscious state was her dragging me into my reading room in the basement, next to the fireplace. Even now I can hear the click of her cane against the floor." The Queen shuddered. "When I came to, it was already a late hour and everyone had gone to the ball."

"Then what did you do?" Victor said, leaning toward her to encourage the Queen on.

"I saw my fairy book lying in the ash, where I had left it. I picked it up, opened it to the page where my Fairy Godmother was painted so clearly, and that is when I remembered my mother's dress and the Godmother's glass slippers. I thought for sure, they would bring me luck.

"And did they?"

"Absolutely," the Queen said as she batted her eyes at the King.

"I ran as quickly as I could up to my room and changed into my dress and slippers."

"I have no doubt that you were stunning," Victor said, almost flirting.

"She was indeed," said the King, chiming in.

"After you were dressed, how on earth did you get to the ball? The Countess and her girls had already left in the carriage," said Victor.

"That was the most amazing part of the evening. I was prepared to walk all the way to the castle but when I stepped out of the house the most enchanting coach was waiting for me."

"This could not be the famous pumpkin carriage, could it?"

"The very one. I had never seen its equal in craftsmanship or stature. It was small enough that only I could fit into it, but I rested comfortably on the finely-cushioned seat. And yes, it was shaped like a pumpkin. I knew then that my Godmother was watching over me.

"Before I knew it, I was whisked off to the castle."

"Who was driving this fine coach for you?"

"Who do you think?" she barked at the impertinence of the question.

Victor turned and looked at Claire with a sly expression on his face. Walking away from the Queen toward Claire he said, "I am sorry, Your Mejesty, I did not mean to interrupt your thoughts. Please continue."

"When the carriage pulled up to the front gate I said that I would be back by midnight. Everyone else would be getting out of the ball closer to one and I wanted time to make it home before my stepmother arrived."

"Fascinating."

"The party began long before I got there. I was sure that I had already missed the dancing, when, out of nowhere, a kind man came up to me and asked me to dance."

She gestured to the King. King Fabian rose. "I had been introduced to so many boorish people all night," he said, moving towards the Queen. "Including your stepsisters."

The King took her hand in his and kissed it. "But when this blushing beauty stepped into the back of the room, I noticed her immediately. So immediate that when I rushed up to her, I do not think she even knew who I was."

The Queen batted her eyes. "Not many girls are asked to dance by such a handsome man."

"You are not just any girl, my dear. You are my wife."

"You did not know that then," the Queen argued.

Victor stepped back and allowed the King and Queen to reenact their night of dancing.

"What happened next?" Victor asked, not allowing them to get too wrapped up in their nostalgia.

"What did happen next?" the King repeated, trying to recall.

"The clock bell rang," said the Queen, reminding him.

"Yes, that dreadful clock bell," said the King, and then looked at Victor. "I had the bells removed shortly after that night."

Gossip

The Queen put a finger on his lips to silence him. Her smile slowly faded as the memory took hold. "I broke away from him. All I remember saying is, 'I have not met the Prince yet.' Bang—one, two, three...

"He tried to say something to me but all I could hear were the bells ringing. So I ran. I ran as quickly as I could while the bells continued to scream at me. Four, five, six...

"I moved through the ballroom and the entrance hall. Seven, eight, nine.

"I finally made it to the front stair and out the entrance gate to my small pumpkin carriage. The door was already open, ready for my great escape. But I was startled by all of the voices shouting behind me."

"I tried to get them to stop you. I did not want you to get away," the King confessed.

The Queen did not break from her trance to acknowledge what the King had said. "I fell. Not hard, but enough that my body hit the ground. I staggered to my feet and continued forward. I could hear the loud shouting starting to blend in with the bells. Ten, eleven. Everything was upon me. Then... twelve."

The Queen looked up at Claire and locked eyes with her. "I made it. I was back in my carriage, rushing home. I did not realize until I got out of the carriage that my slipper was missing."

The King moved to the Queen's side and grabbed her hand again. "I sent her slipper with the magistrate to all the ladies of the land in search of her."

"That could have taken quite some time, Your Highness. How did you find her so quickly?" Victor asked.

"To this day, I do not know how he got through the gate, but this beggar came in and said he knew where I could find my mysterious guest."

"A beggar told you this? And you believed him?"

"I was so desperate to find her, I did not care who told me," admitted the King. "Besides, I have found him to be a trustworthy advisor ever since."

Victor looked back at Claire, not understanding. Then, the King pointed to the Captain.

"Captain Michael Blanc."

The Captain stepped forward proudly.

"Michael?" Claire repeated.

"Michael is my first name," the Captain said and glared at her with a knowing look.

"I see," said Claire, starting to put more pieces together.

"You see?" the Queen quickly followed.

Claire didn't respond. Her eyes were looking the Captain over as the story Genevieve told earlier was coming back to her. An odd silence fell throughout the room.

"Well?" shouted the Queen.

Victor threw his hands up, gesturing to both the King and Queen. "She sees that the Countess could never be telling us the truth about you. Your Mejesty, you are a fine woman and you have found your king. I am very happy for you both."

"Thank you," the Queen said, a little breathless. "Now that you have met me and heard my side, I believe that you will see my stepmother in a new light."

Breaking from her trance, Claire stepped forward. "Meeting you has certainly put things into perspective for me."

The King and Queen made their way back to their seats. A squire rushed out with a bowl of hot water and the Queen washed her hands ceremoniously like she had done the night before.

Once she was finished, she stated, "Now, I wish for you to pack your things and leave from the Countess' estate immediately. If you do not, I will make things very difficult for you both."

Victor and Claire bowed. "Understood, Your Mejesty."

"Captain, please show them out," said the King.

"Yes, Your Mejesty."

The Captain and the two foreigners quickly made their way across the room and out the main doors.

Chapter 17
"The Masked Ball"

Claire looked curiously at the Captain as he sat down in the carriage across from Victor and her before it started its journey back to the Countess' home.

"Why did you not tell me you are Michael?" Claire questioned.

"You did not ask," the Captain said simply, looking out the window at the castle.

"You did not go to the masked ball to get reacquainted with Paris. You went to get reacquainted with Genevieve."

"Are they not one in the same?" He looked directly at Claire. She could now see the years of torment resting uneasily in his eyes.

"Which one of you is going to enlighten me on what is going?" said Victor, cutting in.

"This is the man that Genevieve asked me to help her find. The Captain and she have been in love since they were children. The Countess separated them and now he is back to get Genevieve," explained Claire. "Did I miss anything?"

The Captain shook his head.

"Thank you for clearing all that up for me," replied Victor, unmoved. "Please continue with your discussion."

Claire leaned toward the Captain. "Are you coming with us to the Countess'?"

"The King and Queen did want me to see you out. I do believe they meant the country, not just the castle."

"Of course they did," Victor said, nudging Claire in the arm. "Claire is the biggest threat to France since England."

The Captain stared blankly at Victor, and then shifted his attention to Claire. "How is it that the Countess brought you here?"

Claire stared back at him questioningly, but then slid her hand into her satchel and rummaged around in it. Finally she produced a small envelope with the Countess De Leon's seal on the outside.

"I want to read this to you, but you have to understand that there is some very sensitive material in here that I do not wish to be common knowledge" said Claire.

The Captain took her hand in confidence. "You have my word."

Claire could feel the weight of Victor's disapproving eyes. She slowly slid her hand out of the Captain's. Pulling the letter from the envelope she read:

Dear Mademoiselle Du Bois, or should I address you as Baron C. Dupree?

If you have not realized by the seal on the envelope, I am the Countess De Leon, the Queen's very own evil stepmother. It has been quite some time since I have spoken to anyone outside my estate, so do forgive me if I am brief. I would very much appreciate it if you came to visit me here at my home on Saturday next.

I believe I can tell you things that would peak the interest of even the dullest mind. I will explain myself further upon your arrival. Know that you are the only one I will talk to. Otherwise, my secrets will accompany me to my grave.

I do hope you come. I have been looking forward to meeting you ever since I have learned of your identity. Especially because, whether you know it or not, you have quite a past here in France. One I am very sure you would like to know more about. See you Saturday next.

*Sincerely,
The Countess De Leon*

Upon finishing, Claire folded the letter back up neatly into the envelope and returned it to her satchel.

"She is a fierce creature," the Captain acknowledged.

"She has to be after all she has been through," Claire countered. "Now it is I who has a question for you, Captain."

The Captain bowed his head for her to continue.

Reaching back into her satchel, Claire pulled out the emerald ring. "I noticed the Queen became very agitated when she saw this last night. She would not say what it was about this ring that bothered her so, but she was clearly upset by its presence."

The Captain took it from her and examined it closely. "I do not recognize it, nor do I recall her ever mentioning it before."

"Green is the color all love in their sight, but not she who hates it with all her spite," Claire uttered. She too, was scrutinizing the ring that rested perfectly in the Captain's hand.

"Josephine said that when she handed the ring to me. I believe that she was referring to the Queen."

"Josephine is out of her mind," Victor scoffed.

"I disagree. She seems to know things, it is just—no one can seem to completely understand her riddles."

Victor rolled his eyes until they looked out the window at the dense forest the carriage was moving through.

"Mademoiselle Du Bois, you will not have much time with the Countess upon your return," the Captain noted. "I will be back with my guard shortly, to see you out."

A prolonged silence fell as Claire continued to look at the ring.

"Then we will need to hurry," she said, with understanding.

"We will return in the morning, and if you have not presented by then . . ."

"What? You will arrest us?" said Victor, annoyed.

"No, we will arrest—"

"—The Countess," Claire finished.

The carriage came to a halt. Botley was waiting just outside for them. The old butler's face remained ever-pleasant as he opened the door and helped Claire out.

Botley looked into the carriage. "Captain, it has been some time since you have been here."

From what Claire could see, the Captain's eyes popped. "I know."

Botley's head shifted to Victor. "Monsieur Krouse."

Victor began to get out when the Captain grabbed his arm and whispered something in his ear. Claire couldn't make it out but saw Victor's lips curve into a contented smile.

After Victor hopped out of the backseat, the Captain leaned toward Botley. But as his lips parted, Botley cut him off, "Good day, Captain." Then shut the door in his face.

"What did the Captain say to you?" Claire whispered to Victor with curiosity.

Victor kept his eyes on the carriage as it made its way off the grounds. "Nothing of importance."

"Victor Krouse, I know that smirk you gave. He must have said something to you-"

No more could be said because Botley turned to face them. The pleasantness he had displayed moments earlier was now replaced with a disapproving look.

"The Countess would like to speak to both of you," Botley said, distress lingering in his voice.

"I am sure she would," said Claire. "I do have a few questions of my own."

As Botley brushed past her, he said, "She thought you might."

* * *

"I told you not to leave this estate, did I not?" the Countess scolded them.

Sitting in her chair, the Countess dropped an envelope with the royal seal on the desk in front of Claire.

Claire quickly scooped it into her hands and read it out loud.

To the Countess De Leon,

I am quite aware of the unwanted guests staying with you. By unwanted guests, I mean they are your guests and I do not want them there. They are to leave immediately from your residence. Failure to do so will result in punishment.

Sincerely,
Queen Isabella

Claire's eyes shot up to the Countess. The refined woman pulled out her hand-carved pipe and lit it.

"Do you think she is serious?" Claire asked.

"You already know the answer to that question."

Victor stepped in, "You do not seem too troubled by the news."

"Isabella has been wanting an excuse to lock me up for years. Now she has one," the Countess sighed. "The only reason I brought you up here is because I am sure you have more questions for me."

"I do," Claire jumped on the statement.

The Countess gestured with her hand for Claire to ask.

"I really want to know about the night of the ball. We started talking about it before I had to go to the castle. I would like you to finish."

Taking a few puffs from her pipe, the Countess leaned back in her chair, her fingers interlacing one another.

"I told Isabella she could go that night to the ball. After all, she was an eligible woman with good fortune. But when the time came to leave, she was nowhere to be found."

Claire's eyes searched the room and finally landed on the Countess' cane leaning against the wall.

"Did you even try to look for her?"

"What was the point? I have never seen a girl disappear so much. I figured she had changed her mind. So, Josephine, Genevieve, and I left.

"The ball was quite grand. I even saw the spot where Count Daughtry slid that silly carnation over my shoulder. Being there after so many years brought back many memories, most of which I was not prepared for.

"I quickly rushed the girls into the entrance hall, not wanting to get caught up in times past. A long line of women stood in the middle of the ballroom. One by one they were being introduced to Prince Fabian. If he liked them, he would present them with a rose and would dance with them later that evening.

"However, looking around the room, I noticed that not a single girl had received a rose. I could almost swear that I saw the Prince yawn a time or two. This did not instill a whole lot of confidence in me that my girls would be any different.

"The night wore on and the line thinned when music began to play. People started dancing throughout the room but not one of them with the Prince. I watched him closely. He did not seem to like any kind of girl, because girls of all shapes and sizes came before him. I think, now, that he was just trying to defy his father.

"Anyway, the Prince sat on his throne watching the festivities when something caught his eye. He moved quickly across the room to a corner. The music stopped and people watched him. A girl, who was hard to distinguish with all the people impeding my view, had wrapped her arm inside the Prince's and they began to dance.

"I could hear the gossip fly like wildfire through the court, 'Who is this girl?'

"I, too, wondered the same question until my eyes landed on the glass slippers. I think my heart skipped a beat. I could not confirm that that was indeed Isabella before the two disappeared out to a private balcony."

"The Queen did tell us a very similar story, though, I believe she thinks you never noticed her," Claire said.

"Who could not notice her? She was the first girl the Prince even paid attention to."

"Did you see her at the castle again that night?"

"No, I did not. After the party, I went home to find her door locked. I thought for sure I just imagined the whole thing."

"Understandable if you saw her for only a second . . ." Victor pointed out.

"It was not until the next morning when a squire and the Magistrate showed up at my front door with the glass slipper that I knew I was not wrong in believing Isabella was there that night.

"They asked if my daughters would try on the shoe, though they take after their father in having big feet. They asked me if any other ladies were in the house. I said 'no' because I thought for sure that Isabella would be out in the woods washing her dress.

"But when the Magistrate made his way to the door, Isabella's voice rang through the room. 'Here I am.' They turned to see the ash-covered girl making her way down the stairs.

"'Who might I ask is this?' the Magistrate asked me. 'Cinderella!' I gasped, confusing her name with the cinders she was covered in."

"Did you trip the squire on his way to Isabella?" Claire asked.

"Excuse me?" the Countess exclaimed, a little taken aback. "What kind of preposterous question is that?"

"It is just, as I have heard the story told to me, it sounded like the slipper was broken when you supposedly took your walking stick and tripped the squire."

The Countess lit her pipe once again. Smoke danced from her lips as she exhaled, "No doubt you have met my daughter, Josephine."

Both Claire and Victor quickly nodded at the question.

"She has this ability to lose control of her body, mostly in the act of twirling. Well, when the squire was walking towards Isabella, Josephine collided with him, knocking him over. She meant nothing by it but the shoe was already smashed on the floor.

"Isabella loves that moment because she knew she would be queen as soon as she presented the other slipper to the Magistrate. I knew then that my life would never be the same."

Silence fell in the room.

"The Queen said you hit her that night before the ball. That is why she never made it to the carriage."

"She can think what she wants and if she wants to believe I hit her, then I guess I did."

"I saw the scar on her head," said Victor.

The Countess looked away. "It is of no consequence to me now. You will be heading back to Stuttgart in the morning and I will be going to prison."

"You do not know that," strained Claire. "We can be out of here before night fall."

The Countess held up her hand to stop Claire from saying another word.

"It does not matter if you leave tonight or in the morning. Isabella has her mind made up. Besides, you are not done here. Now that you have heard my story in its entirety, you will be given access to everything."

"Everything?" Claire asked excitedly.

"Everything. Now, if you have no further questions, I think you should go."

The Countess rose, almost shooing them out of the room.

But before Claire made her way fully out of the door, she turned back and said, "How long have you known King Fabian was my brother?"

The Countess still did not look at Claire. "As long as I have known your identity."

And with that the Countess shut the study door in Claire's face and locked it.

Chapter 18
"The Secret Artist"

The stairwell was damp and moldy. Rats could be heard scurrying along the rocks in dark crevasses along the wall. Cold air blew down the circular stair. This time, Botley was not waiting for Claire on the other side of the door as she had originally anticipated.

When Victor and Claire finally took the last step, the door was slightly ajar. The light coming from within the room highlighted the pumpkin etched into the wood.

"Ha!" Victor screamed and grabbed Claire's side.

"Ah!" Claire said jolted. "Victor! Why do you do that?"

Victor chuckled, pleased with himself. "Twenty years of bad habits, I guess."

Claire rolled her eyes and then took a step into the room.

Unlike the last time Claire had been in the tower, the room was in disarray around the quiet Josephine, who was sitting on the edge of the bed.

The wardrobe had been overturned and a large pile of clothes spilled out in front of it. The writing desk sat wide open and pieces of parchment with drawings trickled throughout the room.

Claire walked carefully over to the bed, trying not to disturb Josephine, and sat down next to her.

As Claire looked closer, she seemed to be drawing.

"What do you think happened here?" Victor asked.

Claire picked up one of the many pictures that were piling up on the floor at Josephine's feet. The picture was of Isabella washing her dress in the river and Josephine kneeling next to her, holding out a bar of soap.

"It is hard to say when Josephine is around. It looked nothing like this the last time I was up here."

Victor walked over to the wardrobe and lifted it from the floor. Claire quickly moved over to help him, leaving Josephine to draw quietly on the bed.

As Claire sifted through the pile of shabby clothes, a single article of clothing emerged in her hand: a pale blue, beaded ball gown that looked like it had been worn several times.

Claire held it out to take a better look. "I think this is the dress she wore that night."

Victor snickered at the dress. "Why would she not have it with her at the castle?

"She was taken immediately to the castle upon her discovery," Claire said.

"She could have come back for her things."

"Maybe she wanted to forget this part of her life," Claire suggested.

She delved deeper into the pile of clothes to see what other treasures she would find when she felt a sharp pinch. Looking down, some unknown object pierced the tip of her finger and a little stream of blood trickled out.

"Here," Victor said, ripping a piece of cloth and tightly wrapping it around her hand.

When her eyes met his, a great affection rested in them. "Thank you," she said awkwardly.

She returned to searching through the pile of clothing to discover the sharp object that caused her cut. She pulled out a small shard of glass and held it up victoriously. Her face was almost beaming.

"Do you know what this is?"

Victor looked at the shard quizzically and shrugged his shoulders at it, not understanding.

Claire's hand went back into the pile. "If I remember the Countess' story correctly, the shoe was still intact."

Claire pulled out the glass slipper. It was made of fine silk with small beads and a cracked glass heel. "I cannot believe this is the infamous glass slipper."

"Dumpy dumm dumm. Dumpty dumm dumm. Hmmm hmm hmm hmmmmm," burst from Josephine's lips.

Claire and Victor looked at each other, nervously.

Slipping the broken shoe and the shard of glass into her satchel, Claire sat back down next to Josephine on the bed.

"Josephine?"

Josephine looked at Claire but her hands didn't stop drawing. Stroke after stroke, the image of Isabella sitting in a windowsill formed on the paper. Then, Josephine added herself to the portrait, combing Isabella's hair.

"This is amazing," Claire muttered to herself. "How can you do this?"

"Long is love from the sky above. As you know a friend from beginning to end."

"Did you know her from beginning to end? Isabella?"

Gossip

Josephine dropped the finished picture onto the floor and started scrawling on another piece of parchment. This time, she looked forward as she drew. Her eyes seemed to be surveying the room. The image of Isabella falling down danced from the quill as Josephine's hand flicked quickly across the paper. She continued to look out at the room.

Claire delved into her satchel and produced the emerald ring. "Josephine, you said something to me when you handed me this ring."

Josephine kept her focus on the room, still aimlessly looking around.

"Green is the hated color by she who did not love the owner of thee."

Claire's brow furrowed as she tried to recall back to that night in the dining room.

"Is that not what you said in the carriage?" Victor asked.

"Yes, she said it to me in the dining room-"

"Green is the hated color by she who did not love the owner of thee," Josephine repeated, louder, and pushed Claire's hand with the ring in it away from her.

All of a sudden the quill dropped from Josephine's hand and the paper fell to the floor. Her breathing grew heavy and she lunged toward the pile of clothes where Victor was standing.

"What is wrong, Josephine?" Claire asked caringly.

Josephine slowly turned and looked at her, and then turned back to the pile of clothing.

"AHHHH!" Josephine squealed.

Claire covered her ears, as did Victor. "Victor, go get Botley! Quickly!"

Josephine fell onto the pile of clothes, kicking and screaming.

"What is it, Josephine?"

Josephine picked up a piece of Isabella's clothing and threw it across the room. Claire moved beside her and wrapped her up in her arms.

"Shhh. It is all right. I am here. Tell me what is wrong."

"She said I was good! This friend of mine. But she left me all the same. So she could wine and dine. She did not love me at all. This friend of mine. Now I am left here all alone. That is far from fine. Ahhh!"

Josephine stood up and grabbed a hold of the wardrobe and knocked the whole thing over with one mighty pull. Claire heaved her whole body sideways before the wardrobe landed right on top of her.

"Stop it, Josephine! Josephine!" Claire screamed.

Josephine clenched her eyes tightly shut, clutched her ears, and started singing loudly.

Claire stood back, baffled, watching the crazed girl sway back and forth, singing at the top of her lungs. Before she knew what was going on, Botley was next to Josephine holding a small tonic bottle.

He poured it into Josephine's mouth and covered her lips with his hand. She squealed and hit Botley hard in the chest repeatedly.

"Swallow."

"MMMM," Josephine struggled.

"Swallow!"

Josephine choked down the tonic. It took only a moment longer of struggling before her whole body went limp.

"Have you seen enough?"

"What did you do to her?" Claire asked, concerned.

Botley pulled Josephine into his arms and glared at Claire. "Calmed her. Now, if you will excuse me."

The old butler picked up Josephine's limp body and made his way down the stairwell.

Victor came up behind Claire and patted her on the shoulder. "I think we should go."

Claire's eyes fixed on the bed where Josephine had been sitting.

"Claire," Victor urged.

Claire shook her head, waking from her trance. She collected all the pictures that Josephine had drawn. Tucking them under her arm and heading out to the stairwell, she said, "The story is here. I just know it."

Chapter 19
"Puzzle Pieces"

The early morn was breaking when a loud BANG caused Claire's eyes to pop open. She was still fully clothed and lying on the floor. Next to her was a chaise that had all of Josephine's pictures strewn across it. For a moment she thought she was still dreaming, but then she heard another BANG followed by the sound of low voices.

Claire instantly hopped to her feet and ran to the window that overlooked the front grounds of the estate. Using her cane to help her, the Countess was being led by two armed guards into the back of a carriage.

Before she knew it, Claire was running out of her bedroom. Botley was waiting in the entrance hall, as calm as ever.

"They took her?" Claire gasped.

"I guess the Queen really did want you to leave immediately."

"This is ridiculous!" Claire hissed.

A smile crept up under Botley's mustache. "The Countess thought you might say that."

The old butler held out a letter addressed to Mademoiselle Du Bois.

Claire snatched it from his hands and looked at it closely. "I hope you will excuse me, Botley."

Botley bowed his head to her.

Claire started her ascent up the stairs when Botley called up, "Mademoiselle Du Bois."

She turned to him.

"I hope you do not mind that I told the Countess of last night's events."

"Was she upset?" asked Claire.

"I find that the Countess seldom ever gets upset."

Claire's eyes narrowed in thought and then she continued up the stairs and out of sight.

Upon closing the door to her room, she quickly tore open the envelope and read.

Dear Mademoiselle Du Bois,

Do accept my apology that our time together was so short. I have no doubt that you have already put so much of these puzzle pieces together to tell the disconcerting story that is my life. There are only two pieces left that you need. One is in your possession, the other, only my old butler can tell you. I do appreciate your time in my household, however brief it was. All I can hope now is that you will be able to tell a more accurate tale that has a little less magic and a little more truth.

All My Best,
Countess Desiree De Leon

A knock rapped on her door and Victor entered.

"The Countess was taken into custody by the royal guard," Claire said, still looking down at the letter.

"Well, good morning to you too?"

Her eyes finally lifted to Victor. "There are only two pieces left that you need. One is in your possession . . ." Claire closed her eyes and repeated, "One is in your possession."

Victor looked at her as if she had lost her mind. "What is going on here?"

Claire's lower lip curved into its ever comfortable place under her teeth, then released it and said, "One is in my possession . . . Botley said that he told the Countess about everything that happened last night."

"And?"

"She gave me this letter. It says that I have pretty much all the pieces of the puzzle. The last two remaining pieces reside with myself and with Botley."

"What pieces?" Victor yawned, still not awake yet.

"That is what I am trying to figure out. What do we have? The broken glass slipper, the dress, the emerald ring and . . . Josephine's pictures."

Claire went back to the drawings. "I was looking at them all night. It really does seem like the two girls were good friends, but something happened."

"Is there any sign of what that was?" Victor pondered out loud.

The two looked across the row of pictures laid out. The first drawing was Isabella in her ball gown with Prince Fabian. Then one of the fireplace where Isabella was reading a book and Josephine was playing with figurines on the mantle. The third was the picture of Isabella falling down. The fourth was a cane in someone's hand, and finally was the picture that Claire saw Josephine draw the night before of Isabella sitting on a windowsill with Josephine brushing her hair.

Claire and Victor probed the pictures over and over again.

"We can assume that the pictures of Josephine with Isabella all go together. Then, Prince Fabian. But the picture of the cane is still unsettling."

"Well, that is the only one in which no one is drawn," Victor noted.

"No, that's not what's bothering me."

Claire took the drawing of the cane in her hand and peered closely at it, slowly scratching the surface with her fingernail. She paused.

"What is it?" Victor asked.

"Something I do not understand, Josephine draws with such precision, but she seems to have left an ink blot on this picture."

"Maybe it was just a mistake," Victor offered.

"I doubt it."

Her eyes ran over each picture over and over again until they moved like a play in front of her. Slowly, she started shifting the pictures around.

"What if . . ." Claire muttered to herself and shuffled the pictures around some more.

"And then . . ." The pictures moved again. At last, the pictures lay side by side as she started telling the story to herself.

Every picture was laid out before her in the order she was devising except one. The cane. Claire's eyes ran across Josephine's tale of her time with Isabella. Her eyes jumped picture to picture until they landed on Isabella falling.

"Maybe the Countess hit her with the cane, knocking the Queen out cold," Victor said haphazardly.

Claire's eyes shifted down to the cane then back up to the picture of Isabella falling.

"Victor!" Claire gasped. "You are a genius!"

She quickly kissed Victor on the cheek and then ran out of the room.

"Wait!" screamed Victor. "Nothing like a woman telling you you are a genius then running away from you."

* * *

Claire came barreling down the hall to the Countess' study. She tried to open the door, but it was locked.

"Blast it all," Claire huffed.

"I was wondering when you would make the connection."

Claire turned to see Genevieve standing elegantly to one side of the hall. She pulled out a key ring and took the key needed to open her mother's study.

"You never got to see that painting, did you?"

"That is why I am here."

Before Genevieve opened the door, she turned back to Claire. "Now that you know, you must help her."

"I will do my best."

Genevieve pushed the door to the study open. Claire moved past her through the room to the Countess' desk. Behind it rested the painting that the Countess had turned around the first night Claire was there.

"That is odd," said Genevieve. "She must have taken it down just before you got here."

"She probably wanted to tell me the story first." Claire turned the picture around to reveal the painting of the Fairy Godmother prominently in the middle of the picture and off to the one side was Isabella with Prince Fabian, smiling. On the other side was Josephine crying.

"She really lived in torment, did she not? She has the picture of Count Daughtry's dead wife right outside her office door. She has this picture of Isabella living well while Josephine suffers."

Claire looked back down at the painting of the Fairy Godmother.

"You must go," Genevieve urged.

Claire's eyes flickered up. "Have Botley meet me outside in twenty minutes. Make sure he has the carriage ready."

"I will tell him at once."

"You must go, too," Claire said.

"Me?"

"You and Josephine are an important part of this story."

"But I have not been out in society in years. Neither has she."

Claire looked at Genevieve with a huge smile across her face. "Perhaps it is time to become 'reacquainted' with Paris."

* * *

Botley had the horses hitched up when Claire made her way out of the house. She was the first one of the group to be ready to go. While she waited next to the carriage, Botley gave her a look of disapproval.

"What?" she asked sternly.

"I think if the Countess wanted you to come after her, she would have said something to me about it."

Claire moved agitatedly to the other side and got into the back of the carriage. "If you have not noticed, Botley, she is not exactly the most forthcoming person in the world."

"Maybe with you, Mademoiselle, but with me she is always quite clear of her intentions."

"Now we are following my intentions."

"Clearly," he muttered.

"Where is everyone else?" Claire wondered aloud.

"Try to remember that these girls have been in this house a long time. They might be more nervous confronting their horrible past, than say, you are."

Claire turned away from his rude comment and waited impatiently. Her eyes narrowed before she realized what she was looking at.

"Botley, come with me."

"Mademoiselle?"

Claire climbed out of the carriage and went straight for the side of the house.

Opening the large door into the barn, her eyes scanned the empty stables. "You told me while we were standing in the tower that the Count got a few other things when he got the door with the pumpkin on it."

Claire looked at the old butler and then stepped into the empty barn.

"The pumpkin carriage is not the mad ramblings of the Queen, is it?"

Botley looked at her blankly.

"I know it was you who took Isabella to the ball that night. Please, show me where it is."

The old butler grabbed Claire's hand and pulled her to one side of the barn. Then he kicked a big pile of loose hay away from the floor exposing a large door. With Claire's help he struggled to slide it open. Underneath was a little ramp and a large object concealed beneath a tarp.

Claire moved quickly down into the hole. Pulling the cloth tarp away, the small iron carriage that was shaped like a pumpkin stood before her.

"The pumpkin carriage is real."

Claire shot a look at Botley.

"He died before he could give this to her. Only years later, when she needed to go to the ball and the carriage was already gone, did you think of this. Am I correct?"

"You are right on all accounts," Botley confirmed.

"The Countess is in real trouble," Claire stated.

"The worst part is, I think she has given up the thought that she will ever be left alone. I think she has just been worn down over the years by Isabella," Botley said, and then pulled the tarp back over the carriage.

"I need you to get the girls out here; I truly believe I can save her from her own stepdaughter."

Without any warning, Botley reached out and hugged Claire. There was a sense of comfort and sincerity that caused Claire to accept the embrace. When they finally broke, Claire asked, "What was that for?"

For the first time since they had met, Botley lost his composure. He released a deep sigh, "That is the first kind word this family has heard in . . . well, a long time."

Claire clutched his arms in her hands and looked at him straight-faced. "I hate to see anyone suffer because of a misunderstanding. Now, we must hurry before it is too late."

Botley nodded and scuttled off toward the house.

Chapter 20
"The Cane"

"Are you sure you know what you are doing?" Victor asked as the carriage came to a halt in front of the castle. "Seems last time you were here, you got a little tongue tied."

Claire glanced down at the drawings sitting in her lap, and then over at Josephine. She was pulling at her long stringy hair while she hummed her own little tune to herself.

Claire looked back at Victor's unsure expression. Then she turned to Genevieve who remained quietly looking out the window.

"The Countess will never say what really happened that night. I must say it for her."

"Do you really know what happened or do you just think you know?" questioned Victor.

"She knows," said Genevieve sternly. "However, Mother would never approve of you coming to the castle like this."

"There you go," said Victor. "We should turn around."

"We cannot. Besides, there is more to be gained from this visit than just saving the Countess," argued Claire.

"Like?" Victor said with curiosity.

"When all is done, there is nothing to fear. It is too late for us, the guard is here," hummed Josephine.

The carriage door flew open and four royal guards stood outside with muskets pointed at them.

"All right, all of you out," screamed Monsieur Monte.

"Ah," Victor hummed to Claire. "It is our old friend."

They all came out to the courtyard where more guards awaited them.

"You should have left when you had the chance," the head guard spat.

"Come now, these are the Queen's guests," said a familiar voice.

Genevieve was the first to turn and see the Captain approaching. He smiled at them all but reached out and took Genevieve's hand. Her lips parted and a little gasp escaped. The Captain bowed and kissed her hand.

"My Lady, it has been far too long," he said, then turned to the royal guard and gestured for them to drop their weapons. "I do not think we are in any danger, men. Stand at the ready."

The guards followed their Captain's orders and rested their muskets at their sides.

"Now that you are here, I guess we should take you to the main event. The King and Queen are questioning the Countess as we speak."

"It is strange to me that you are not in there with them." Claire pondered out loud.

"They had a feeling you would not be far behind so they sent me out here to wait for you. Now that you have arrived, I think it only right to show you in."

The Captain gestured with his hand to follow him but before he moved he held out his elbow to Genevieve. She looked at him, bright-eyed and in disbelief, but interlaced her arm with his.

"I thought you were dead," she whispered to the Captain.

"I was until a moment ago," replied the Captain. When he looked over at the blushing beauty, she smiled cordially and then faced forward again.

When the group entered the room, the Countess was standing before the thrones in a very proper manner. Her hands were shackled in front of her and she held her head up high as she spoke. Queen Isabella stood before her, and Claire noticed that she was holding onto the Countess' cane.

"Ah, I thought you would never join us," said the King in a jovial tone.

The group moved through the room until they too were standing in front of the King and Queen. The Queen's sharp eye darted from the group to the Countess.

"Why did you bring these foreigners to your house?" demanded the Queen.

"They are friends," the Countess said tranquilly.

"They are more than that, I think," stated the King. "After questioning them yesterday, I am quite convinced you had them summoned here to contradict the Queen's story. Is that not so?"

The Countess looked up at Isabella. "If by contradict you mean telling them the truth, then yes, I did."

"Blasphemy!" the Queen said, eyes narrowed.

"Is it, Isabella?" the Countess asked, not backing down from the Queen's harsh glare.

"How dare you," hissed the Queen, raising her hand to strike the Countess across the face.

"Isabella, no." said Botley in a father-like tone, calming the tension. "That will not make it right."

Looking back over to the group of traitors, the Queen's eye caught the old butler. "Botley, I had hoped you would not have come with this riff raff, though I am glad you old friend."

The Queen relaxed her hand and moved over to kiss Botley on the cheek. Genevieve, who was still attached to the Captain's side, instantly distracted her. "I should have guessed you would be here, supporting your traitorous mother."

"Lofty words coming from you, now that you are Queen," Genevieve replied ever-so-calmly.

The Queen's face became morose. "Just because I did not say all that was in my mind when I was a child, did not mean I was weak. I was polite. Something, I fear, you have never really known anything about."

Genevieve bowed her head to the Queen mockingly. The Queen's eyes narrowed before turning on to the two foreigners.

Before she spoke, she gestured with her hands and the squire came out with the hot bowl of water and a bar of soap. As Claire had seen previously, the Queen ceremoniously washed her hands while she looked Victor and her over.

"I thought I was quite clear yesterday in asking you to leave immediately," said the Queen.

"I thought it only right for me to stay until I know my friend is out of harm's way." Claire gestured to the refined woman, still unflinching in her conduct.

The Queen, too, looked at the Countess. "You are wasting your time. She is bound for the stocks."

"Please, Your Highness-" Claire pleaded, looking past the Queen to the King.

"That is enough!" The Queen snapped, slamming the cane into the ground. The forceful sound resonated through the room. She stepped toward Claire, "I want you and your friend to leave France at once, never to return. Am I clear enough this time?"

"No." Claire said simply.

Murmurs whispered around the room. The Queen looked at all the questioning faces of the court then back at Claire.

"No?" the Queen repeated, angrily. "I said leave!"

"No."

This time the crowd whispered louder. Hands covered mouths in shock and eyes were wide open, waiting to see how the Queen would handle this defiance.

"What do you mean, no? Guards, come and remove her from the court!"

The Captain released Genevieve, stepped toward the guards with his hand held up to stay in their positions.

"What is the meaning of this?" yelled the King and rose to his feet. All the nobles in the room fell to their knees except the group before them and the Captain.

"Your Mejesty, I have been in your service for many years now. I implore you and the Queen to hear Mademoiselle Du Bois," pleaded the Captain.

"Guards, take the Captain into custody," came the King's reply.

"Escort these two out of France and make sure they stay out," said the Queen. "As for Genevieve, take them to the jail and hold them there until we decide what to do with them."

The guards did as they were ordered and quickly detained all of the members of the group.

"Wait," said Claire. "Your Highness, there is so much you do not know."

"I do not wish to know!" argued the King. "You have done nothing but stir up trouble since you have been here."

"Please, King Fabian-"

"I said, get them out of here!" demanded the Queen.

"Listen to her!" screamed Botley over the crowd.

"Why should I?" said the King, taking lofty steps toward the old butler.

"Because she is your sister."

The room fell silent. The King grabbed Botley by the coat and leaned close to his face. "What did you say?"

"If you cannot see the resemblance, then you are blind."

"You are more brazen than the Captain. Would you like to join the Countess in the stocks?" King Fabian threatened.

"You may send me anywhere you like. That does not change that Claire is your sister."

The King's face hardened. Finally he yelled, "Bring her here."

The guards dragged Claire over to him.

"You are not seriously entertaining this idea, My Lord," said the Queen.

"Silence!" the King hissed.

His face was inches from Claire's. He studied every crevice in her forehead, every freckle on her cheek, until his hazel eyes looked into her hazel eyes. Then, the King's gaze drifted down to the necklace around Claire's neck. When he lifted it and saw the ancient royal emblem, his eyebrows relaxed in acknowledgement.

"How can this be?" he whispered under his breath, stunned. He turned to the Queen in disbelief.

The Queen's patience had run out. "You have your orders. Get them out of here," she screamed.

The guards again grabbed the members of the group and started pushing them toward the door.

The struggle with Josephine became fierce when they tried to grab her. All of a sudden, a piercing scream filled the room. Everyone covered their ears. Claire broke free from the grasp of the guard and ran over to her.

"Tell them, Josephine. Tell the Queen what you were trying to tell us with these pictures. Tell her what really happened the night of the ball."

"No," growled the Countess. "Mademoiselle Du Bois has lost her senses."

The guard grabbed Claire by the wrists. She screamed, "Wait a minute."

The King turned back to the room, still looking stunned, and held up his hand. "Let her speak."

The guards released Claire once more and she moved back to Josephine. "Tell your friend what happened."

Josephine shook her head 'no' back and forth, repeatedly.

"Do not do this, Claire," the Countess yelled.

"Silence, evil witch," snapped the Queen.

"She is not as evil as you think. Look for yourself." said Claire, holding out Josephine's pictures to the Queen. The Queen stared blankly before moving closer to Claire and taking them from her.

Gossip

Flipping through them, the Queen's face became perplexed. "These are pictures from our past. That is all they are. Memories from our past."

"I think they are more than that, Your Highness," Claire said, and then turned back to Josephine.

"Then tell me their significance," demanded the Queen.

"The only one who can help you understand is Josephine," Claire said, encouraging Josephine to speak.

But Josephine's head was dropped and her face was hidden behind the strings of her disheveled hair. An awkward moment of silence passed and Josephine simply hummed to herself.

"What happened those many years ago was my fault," the Countess tried to confess. "I take full responsibility."

"I know it was," the Queen agreed. "Guards, take them all away."

"No!" screamed Claire. "Josephine, you must tell your friend the truth!"

The guard took Genevieve by the arms along with the Captain and began escorting them out. At the same time, the Countess struggled with her cuffed wrists.

"Josephine!" she screamed.

Guards tried to grab Josephine but she continuously slipped from their grasp. She placed her hands on her ears, humming louder and louder as the commotion around her grew more frantic. Finally her lips parted.

"She was there, so pretty in blue. She was there, that is when I knew. She would leave me from what I had seen. She would leave me to become queen."

"Josephine, do not do this!" screamed the Countess, still struggling to reach her daughter.

Josephine didn't falter as she continued to sing. "I did not see my friend say goodbye. For days and nights I would cry and cry."

"Stop!" cried the Countess.

"I took the cane into my hand, I took the cane and hit my friend. I dragged her to a place so dark, it was not a garden, nor a park. But to a place where her fairy dreams ran free, in the smoldering ashes by the fiery sea."

Josephine parted her hair, exposing her face for the first time. The Queen's eyes flooded with horror and she stumbled backward up the small stair.

"I could not bear to see my friend go, that night oh so long ago."

Josephine's legs buckled from underneath her and she collapsed to the floor. The Countess broke from the guards' grip and ran over to her daughter.

"The Countess buried her daughter's secrets under the famous fairy tale to protect Josephine," Claire concluded.

"It cannot be," said the Queen, choking back tears.

"It is obvious; even Josephine professed the truth. See the picture of the cane. There's a dot on the hand. That is Josephine's hand." Claire took Josephine's hand and raised it to show the room the mole on her thumb.

"No," the Queen said in denial.

"The Countess is not so evil as you may think."

"She is," the Queen shouted with a waver in her voice that made her sound uncertain.

"Your Fairy Godmother told you that she would appear the next time you really needed her," Claire recalled back to the Countess' story.

"How could you know that?"

"Remember this?" Claire asked the Queen as she pulled out the broken glass slipper.

Claire held it out so that the Queen could see the priceless item, and then turned to show the whole court.

"It is famous for its uniqueness. But where did the Queen get it from?" she asked the crowd of viewers.

"Her Fairy Godmother!" shouted out one of the court.

"That is right. Her Fairy Godmother," repeated Claire. "And Your Highness, how many women did you have try this tiny shoe on before you found your Queen?"

"Hundreds," the King confirmed.

"Hundreds. And did anyone besides the Queen's foot fit into this shoe?"

"Not one."

"Intriguing," Claire said with a knowing smirk on her face. She walked over to the Countess De Leon and removed her shoe and slipped the glass slipper perfectly onto her tiny foot.

The whole crowd gasped in unison.

Claire turned to the room, "She is not as evil as you have all made her out to be."

"I have had enough!" screamed the Queen, overcome by her anger.

In a fit of rage, the Queen barreled toward Claire, with the cane still tightly clenched in her hand. Claire raised her arms in front of her face to protect herself, but before she could attack, Victor took hold of the Queen's arm and pulled her backward. The King jumped in to help restrain her, keeping her just out of reach of Claire.

"That would not be very becoming of a lady," Victor said in his usual humored tone.

"Grah!" the Queen roared.

"Isabella!" the King said sternly, "You need to take your leave."

The Queen stopped struggling with the King and Victor, yanking both of her hands free from their grips.

"Fine," she shouted, throwing the cane down at the Countess' feet. Then she huffed out of the room through a side door.

Looking back at the King, Claire said, "Your Highness, I am not asking you to welcome the Countess with open arms, but I am asking you to simply let her go home and live the rest of her life in peace."

"Are you always this determined in making your point?" the King asked.

"She sure is," Victor whispered to the King.

"You are no better," the King pointed out to Victor. "I could have you severely whipped for putting your hands on the Queen like that. But, I would do no less if I were protecting my wife."

Victor's eyes settled on Claire, who was kneeling next to the Countess and Josephine, and said with an amused grin, "She is not my wife."

"Hm, pity." the King grunted and then turned his attention back to the room. "Let the Countess and her daughters go! As for you, Captain, I think you have been in charge of the royal guard for long enough."

"Your Mejesty?"

"I have a vineyard on the countryside that would be more suited for you," the King said with a smile and then looked over at Genevieve. "Perhaps you can take up with a wife who will keep you company."

"Yes, Your Highness," said the Captain just before Genevieve came and took his arm.

"As for you," the King stepped closer to Claire and looked once more into her eyes. "I think I knew who you were when I first saw you. I would like to think this will not be the last time we see each other."

He took Claire's hand and kissed it. Claire blushed and admitted, "I should hope not."

"You are always welcome here in France."

Claire bowed. "Might I ask one thing?"

"Please."

"What will become of the Countess? I know the Queen truly despises her."

"The Countess will live the rest of her days out in peace. I will make sure of it personally."

The King kissed Claire's hand before returning to his place on his throne.

"Please tell the Baron Dupree, next time he wants a good story to unearth, find another country to do it in."

"Yes, Your Mejesty," both Claire and Victor said in unison.

"Now, you are all free to go."

The group bowed. Botley grabbed Josephine and they all made their way out of the room.

Chapter 21
"Happy Endings"

Two carriages waited for the group in front of the castle. One was the Countess' carriage and the other was waiting to take Claire and Victor back to Germany.

"That was not how I wanted my story to be told," the Countess scolded Claire. "Still, thank you for saving me, if for no other reason than to be with my daughters."

Claire bowed her head with acceptance.

The Countess took a step toward the carriage when Claire began rummaging through her satchel.

"Countess," she said, pulling her closed hand out of her bag.

The Countess turned toward her. Claire put her hand into the Countess' and released the emerald ring.

"I do believe this belongs to you."

The Countess eyed the ring before sliding it onto her ring finger. "Count Daughtry would be happy to know it is back where it belongs. Thank you for everything, Claire."

Claire smiled at her, though the sternness on the woman's face never wavered.

Gossip

The Countess got into the back of her carriage, leaving the door open for the rest of the party to join her. Botley came up alongside Claire.

"Do you think she is angry with me for explaining about Josephine?" Claire asked him.

"She has been angry ever since I have known her," Botley said simply. "I guess that happens when you lose two husbands during your lifetime."

Claire looked up at him with understanding.

"But for what it is worth," Botley continued. "I think you just made her life a little bit easier. I honestly think the rumors will stop and people will leave her be."

A contented smile crossed Claire's face. "I truly hope so . . . Botley?"

Botley slowly turned to her.

"How did you know?" she asked him.

He looked away for just a moment.

"Know what?" he replied in such a tone that sounded like he understood exactly what she meant.

"In the note from the Countess that you gave me, she mentioned that you knew something that I needed to know. At first I thought it might have been the pumpkin carriage, but now I believe it is something else entirely. So I ask you, how did you know I was the King's sister?"

"Well, you look just like him for a start, and . . ."

"And?" Claire asked softly.

Botley paused.

"The Baron Cortland Dupree."

Claire's mouth fell agape.

"That was the character name I made up for myself anytime I told my daughter stories when she was a child. Naturally, she must have used that name with her own daughter."

Botley scooped Claire's hand into his and squeezed it. Claire's eyes started to tear as the answer to her long-awaited question became clear.

"I will never forgive myself for putting your mother out of my home. She was so headstrong and stubborn, much like you. When I heard she was pregnant with the King's child, I knew that she would never be married properly. She would disgrace our household and our name. A hard year passed. I tried to search for her but never found her."

"Then how did you become the butler for the Countess?"

"Actually, it was Count Daughtry who found me in a tavern in Marseille. I blubbered on about losing my daughter, and having a daughter of his own, he took pity on me and brought me into his home. I was thankful.

"As for you . . . when I learned your identity, I went to the Countess making a pact with her. I told her that I knew who you really were and if she brought you here so I could meet you, you would tell the true tale of what happened with Isabella."

"I am so thankful you did," Claire whispered before wrapping her arms around her grandfather and pulling him tightly to her.

"I have missed you so much, my girl," he said. "You are like your mother in so many wonderful ways."

Victor stepped next to them as the two broke from the embrace. "Why do I get the feeling we will be back here soon?" asked Victor, looking at the two of them.

"I hope you will," Botley said. "You are a good man, Monsieur Krouse. Please take care of Claire for me."

"What a chore you ask of me, Sir," Victor laughed. "I have done it this long, what is a few more years?"

Botley glanced from Victor to Claire with a knowing look. "I believe you are up for the task."

Botley hugged Claire once more and hopped into the carriage with Josephine and the Countess.

Genevieve and the Captain approached them.

"Thank you for finding him for me. I think with the status of Captain and the King's blessing, Mother will allow me to marry Michael now," Genevieve said, tightly squeezing the hand of her newfound prize.

"We do what we can," said Victor, dashingly.

Claire shook her head in disbelief of her friend's ridiculousness and then leaned forward, hugging Genevieve. "I wish you both the utmost happiness."

"Thank you," said Genevieve, before the Captain helped her into the back of the carriage, closing the door behind her.

The Captain turned toward Claire, "You lost the bet, but you already knew that long before you ever came to France."

Claire smiled.

"Do not forget what I said to you," the Captain said, pointing to Victor.

"I will keep it in the back of my mind."

"You do that," said the Captain, before mounting his horse.

The carriage rolled off down the country road with the Captain riding along side headed back to the Countess' estate.

When Claire turned her attention back to Victor, he was standing so perfectly with his ever-present smirk.

"What bet?" he asked.

Claire waved him off as if it were nothing and started for their carriage. Before she could make it two steps,

Victor grabbed her by the frills of her dress and pulled her back to him. He looked deep into her eyes with his head cocked to one side and said, "What bet?"

Claire shook her head. "What did the Captain want you to remember?"

Victor released Claire from his hold and stepped toward the carriage.

"Nothing."

"Hmm," she grunted and then ran after him. "You are so stubborn, Victor Krouse."

Just as she said his name he stopped, causing her to collide into him. They both fell to the ground.

Victor brushed the hair away from Claire's face and leaned in. His warm breath washed over her.

"The Captain thought you liked me," Claire confessed. "I assured him we were just friends, but he decided to make a wager on it."

"And?" Victor said with a smile.

"I guess I lost." Claire half smiled at him. "Now tell me. What did the Captain say to you?"

"He said I should give you something."

"Anything in particular?" Claire inquired.

But before she could get any farther, Victor slid out from underneath her and rose to his feet, dumping her on the ground.

"We should get going before we wear out our welcome around here." he said and helped Claire to her feet.

"You are really not going to tell me what you are supposed to give me?"

"I do not see any point; it is a long ride home and it will just get you all excitable. And once you get excitable, you get all these crazy ideas."

"I really hate you, Victor Krouse."

"And you always will." He pulled Claire tightly to him and kissed her passionately, taking her breath away.

The loving embrace lasted several moments before they broke. He took a step backward and straightened up his jacket. "Are you happy now?"

"Very," she said with a giddy chuckle.

"See."

"What?" Claire scoffed.

"There you go, getting excitable," Victor pointed out.

"What is wrong with that? We have been friends our entire life and now..."

"Crazy ideas forming in your head," Victor said resignedly.

"Marriage is far from a crazy id-" but before she could finish her thought, he thrust his lips forward, kissing her again and hopefully this time leaving her speechless.

CPSIA information can be obtained at www.ICGtesting.com
Printed in the USA
LVOW070158190213

320626LV00034B/2089/P